THE
MA

"...he started to beg for mercy, but in vain." (p. 45)

THE MASTER MASOCHIST

TALES OF A SADISTIC MISTRESS

LEOPOLD VON SACHER-MASOCH

Translation by

Eric Lemuel Randall

Introduction by

Vyvyan Howarth

SENATE

The Master Masochist

Previously published in 1968 by Tallis Press Ltd,
London.

This edition published in 1996 by Senate,
an imprint of Random House UK Ltd,
Random House, 20 Vauxhall Bridge Road,
London SW1V 2SA.

Copyright © Tallis Press Ltd, 1968

ISBN 1 85170 555 4

Printed and bound in Great Britain by
Cox & Wyman, Reading, Berkshire

CONTENTS

Translator's Foreword

LEOPOLD VON SACHER-MASOCH was born in 1836, in Lemberg, Galicia, and it was in 1895 that he was finally declared insane and put away in Mannheim asylum, where it is generally believed he died very shortly afterwards.

He had indisputable talent as a writer, but I myself would not go along with those literary commentators of his day who compared him with Russia's Turgenev and even with Germany's Goethe—(had it not been for his 'one-track mind' concerning his 'cruel women' theme). He does certainly have a felicitous turn of phrase and a general economy of words that make him a competent narrator and (considering he lived in an age of turgid verbosity) remarkable for the clarity and vividness of his descriptions.

But, quite apart from the obsession that manifestly clouded his intellect and carried him away (like de Sade a century earlier) into realms of unreal and even grotesque imaginings, he evinces muddled thinking amounting from time to time to flagrant contradiction of fact or time or place, and his wild exaggerations are, like those of de Sade, sometimes too much for the most sympathetic reader to swallow. Allowance has also to be made for the flimsiness of his plots, with their fairy-tale unoriginality. Readers will be struck, I think, by a ring of familiarity in the character of Vlasta and her treatment of the blacksmith's beautiful young wife (in THE WILD HUNTRESS) and will find themselves reminded of the wicked queen in the story of SNOW-WHITE AND THE SEVEN DWARFS; and Sarolta's conduct in murdering Prince Parkany and attributing the killing to his innocent groom (in THE HYENA) is all too reminiscent of the infamous Lady Macbeth.

To all this there must be added two other drawbacks for the modern reader and the translator—his occasional long and complicated German constructions, and his almost prudish avoidance of direct reference to things (like certain parts of the body), and situations, which were unmentionable in published form in the Europe of his day.

He was, for all his depravity, what we should call in England a Victorian. Hence, a row of asterisks very often conceals what a modern reader would regard as the most entertaining or titillating part of the story: too much in too many cases is left to the reader's imagination.

I have done my best to surmount these difficulties, by translating fairly freely, breaking up the heavy German constructions wherever possible to make them more palatable and more digestible to the English-speaking reader. I have also, in most cases, compared other versions (in French) with the original German text, so as to derive what benefit I could from Gallic adaptation— except where the French variation is a manifest mistranslation of the original.

Clearly, however, there is a serious limit to what a translator may permit himself to do. He may attempt to modernise the conversation a little, but not to such an extent that it is absurdly out of context. He may not make the women talk like mini-skirted jet-set floozies when they wear muffs and veils and trailing dresses that only rarely reveal their ankles! I hope the purists will forgive me for the moderate liberties I *have* taken.

Finally, a word of appreciation for the quite excellent 'Explanatory Preamble' by my friend Dr Vyvyan Howarth. I must say that with unabashed frankness the subject of sadomasochism has been laid bare in this exceptional introduction in a manner that fully compensates for Sacher-Masoch's occasional squeamishness. Furthermore, I myself have never seen this difficult and baffling theme so lucidly explained. Some of Dr Howarth's observations, particularly those regarding the relationship between sadism, cruelty, hate and resentment, provide, for what is to me at any rate *the first time ever*, a readily understandable approach to perversions that have been called 'by far the most prevalent anomalies in the sexual life of our time.'

E.L.R. July, 1968

An Explanatory Preamble

BY DR VYVYAN HOWARTH

'CASE No 27: N.L.—married woman, aged 28, slim, beautiful, with well-defined features; wife of highly-placed aristocrat. Spends most of each year leading blameless life on an estate situated near a small town. None of her acquaintances or visitors has slightest suspicion of her secret weakness or the passion she gives way to. Her husband suspects nothing either. But in fact she cannot bear to spend more than half of each year with him, although he dotes on her and grants her everything she wants. She feels compelled to spend the other half of each year at some luxury hotel or a private nursing home on the Riviera or in Switzerland. It has to be in some large house where a substantial number of people forgather in relaxed circumstances...'

This is a rough translation of the beginning of clinical notes recorded by Dr Wilhelm Stekel in his excellent book *Sadism and Masochism**, in which he tells of this patient who, among many other interesting cases that came to him for treatment, consulted him because she wanted him to find a cure for her strange perversity, from which she was anxious to be released—'at any price whatever'. She was afraid her reputation and her social position were in jeopardy. At the last nursing home she had stayed at, a woman in the next room had heard the cracking of the whip she was using on her male victim and had evidently spied on her through the keyhole. The next day the Director had ordered her to leave immediately. She feared her husband might get to hear about it. She had been told that people could be 'changed' by hypnosis. 'I want

---

* *Sadism and Masochism*, The Psychology of Hatred and Cruelty, by Wilhelm Stokel, M.D.

9

to be a normal, healthy woman . . . ' she assured Dr Stekel.

This woman told Stekel that on the very first day at the nursing home she would have a good look at all the people present at the table and make up her mind at once who would be her likeliest victim. He goes on to record his conversation with her: -

'Do you mean which of the men will fall in love with you?'

'No, I mean nothing of the kind. Fall in love?—that is just so much nonsense. Not at all. I am a sadist. I look for the man I am going to whip . . .'

'And can you always find him at a glance like that? Haven't you ever been in a nursing home where you couldn't find one?'

'I always do find one. Generally I find several. I have never yet been in a nursing home where I have not found at least one partner . . . I look them all over one by one. My first glance is serious, merciless, stern. Then in several of the men I notice a cringing response, which I recognise at once! "This man will be my slave!" I say to myself when I have made my selection.'

'And how do you become acquainted?'

'That's never difficult. Sadists and masochists have a secret language, so to speak,—a secret society, one might say, with secret customs and secret intimations. We get into conversation after the meal, and generally make our first date there and then. Of course, we don't mention a word about what we are going to do. I say to him sternly: "Come to my room tonight at nine o'clock!" (or ten o'clock or whatever hour seems convenient to me). I look at him imperiously and stride away. If he wants to detain me and go on talking, I just shake him off as a bitch would get rid of an importunate dog.'

'And does he come?'

'He certainly does—punctually at the specified hour. He never fails to turn up! Then I make him take all his clothes off. I myself remain dressed. Nor will I allow him to make any advances or to kiss me. He simply has to obey: he does so, stripping himself completely and throwing himself at my feet. I hit him with my riding-crop as hard as I can and for as long as I like, taking care not to make a noise that might be heard by others. He groans with pain, or pleasure, and squirms at my feet. Oh, I have seen grovelling in this way proud, famous men, men who were leading lights in their profession, kissing my shoes in gratitude for the blows. I go on thrashing till the blood runs.'

'Does this give you a great pleasure?'

'Of course! But I feel an even more intense satisfaction later when the man flings himself upon me and tries to possess me. Ho, then I give him a withering look and laugh in his face! I watch him contemptuously as passion makes him writhe and desire robs him of every vestige of masculine dignity. He pleads with me, whimpering some flattering gibberish, begging me to let him have me. I remain cold and unmoved, and it is this moment of triumph that gives me more pleasure than I have ever experienced in normal intercourse with my husband.'

'Does he go away without having possessed you?'

'Invariably!'

'Have you never come across a man who would not give in?'

'Oh, yes. Several have tried it on, first cringing with pain and then trying to be virile and using manly strength. Poor fools! They hadn't a hope. I was stronger than they, but I threatened to scream if necessary and so disgrace them. Some I have whipped out of the room and forbidden ever to come back. Believe me, after that these men ran after me like dogs. I could have done anything I liked with them. They were completely in my power.'

'Have you yourself ever succumbed to your own desire?'

'By desire you mean desire for sexual intercourse, I suppose. No. This desire, as you call it, doesn't exist for me any more. Oh, I have intercourse with my husband still, and sometimes with other men; but what feeble pleasure that gives compared with the indescribable bliss of the sadistic act I have described! Then my orgasm reaches intensity that simply could not possibly be greater.

My whole personality is uplifted; I am proud and elated; I am made aware of my tremendous power. My experience is that one cannot have this absolute power over a man if one once surrenders to him. On the other hand, these men are my slaves and run after me still, because they are consumed with passionate desire for me but have never possessed me; because they have come to know how severe I can be and long to find out what it would be like if I were to be tender with them . . . . '

The remarkable book from which this case-history excerpt is taken was written in the nineteen-thirties and appeared not long before the insanities of Fascism and Nazism erupted in the second world war. The confessions of Frau N. L. might be those of any one of a dozen of Sacher-Masoch's women characters. Yet the stories in which they appear, the stories in the book to which these comments of mine form a preface, were penned half a century earlier, by a man who knew nothing about psychoanalysis or psychiatry or the kind of researches into abnormalities that men like Stekel have undertaken, and who, we may be sure, never for a moment suspected that his illustrious name would be requisitioned by the medical profession and perpetuated throughout the world to designate a sexual perversion.

What exactly is masochism? Or, more precisely, what is sadomasochism?—for, as we shall see, sadism and masochism are twin poles of a "bi-polar" phenomenon (to use Stekel's own terminology) and, though in some respects are contrasts, are at the same time inextricably related.

Basically, as the sub-title of Stekel's book suggests, sadomasochism is a hate mechanism: hatred and cruelty are invariably linked, even when no overt acts of violence result. This gives us the clue at once as to why the masochist is also a sadist, though the sadist is not necessarily masochistic. The masochist's hate is inwardly directed: he or she is himself or herself the object of the hate (i.e. he despises himself), and therefore the desire to be cruel is reflexive. (If, for convenience, I refer henceforward to male masochists, the reader will understand that, except to the extent that I shall specifically indicate otherwise, the same comments will apply to women masochists also). The masochist who offers himself to another for punishment is, sexually at least, a coward, and that is why he will seek to induce another (usually of opposite sex) to ill-treat him. Sacher-Masoch went to considerable lengths to persuade his various women to be cruel to him. From the masochist's point of view, although it is clearly an "advantage" if the tormentor is a sadist this need not of necessity be the case.

If we bear in mind that hate springs from resentment, again it becomes easier to understand the connexion and interrelation between sadism and masochism. The woman sadist is resentful because she is not a man, and her resentment makes her adopt the protective armour of regarding herself as superior to any man.

The female masochist is resentful because she *is* a woman, accepts her status as inferior and worthless, and submits to being belittled more and more. It is as though she hates herself for belonging to "the weaker sex" and surrenders soullessly to man's dominance as a punishment and atonement for her abjection. This explains why many writers on the subject have assumed that masochism is basically a woman's role.

The male sadist, who finds her such a willing victim, is obsessed with his masculine superiority, and in consequence hates and despises others' weakness. His belief in his male supremacy may, however, be the result of impotence, or a predisposition to homosexuality, so that in fact his illusion of strength is a compensation-mechanism. Everyone is familiar with the man who is henpecked by his wife at home and is officious and domineering outside his domestic environment, whenever he gets the chance to assert himself. A person with a so-called "inferiority complex" is generally insufferably opinionated and vain, in an unconscious attempt to redress his deficiencies.

Male sexual impotence and suppressed homosexuality may lead to cannibalism and to necrophilia,—that is, to the defiling or mutilation of female corpses. Defloration mania is another familar manifestation. Sometimes such conditions conduce to sexual murder, such as those perpetrated by Neville George Heath some twenty-three years ago: Heath ripped up the genitals of the two girls he murdered, bit off the nipples of their breasts, slashed them with a sharp knife or razor, and rammed objects up their vaginal passages—most of these atrocities being committed while the victims were still alive. The pages of police dossiers all over the world are all too commonly stained with the records of human monsters of this kind, from "Jack the Ripper" and Landru (who was estimated to have murdered about 300 women) to the "Moors Murders" and the crimes of Cannock Chase. Fiction, too, particularly since the first World War, abounds with descriptions of such crimes. Magnus Hirschfeld gives details of a case of sexual murder, which again throw light on the demoniacal hate-mechanism of the impotent sadist (in this case a police sergeant) who commits such murders:-

'In the charge presented to the State Attorney . . . both women, Ella H. and her mother, Ella T., were the victims of a sexual murderer. This conclusion was evidently drawn from the fact that in both cases the genitals were exposed. Frau H. was only covered with a blanket and a towel over her chest, and was completely naked, most of her clothing having been found under her back.

'The shoes and stockings of the murdered woman were scattered all over the kitchen. When the blanket and the bloody towel had been removed, a knife was found to be buried in her left breast, with half an inch of the haft protruding. On the right breast there was a wound evidently caused by biting. There was a wire loop round the corpse's throat. The face at the base of the nose was swollen, apparently from blows with the fist. In the corner of the right eye there was a slight stab wound, while a wound caused by biting was discovered below the right calf.

'In the living-room next to the kitchen lay the body of the murdered Frau T. Her dress was torn from her throat downwards, so that her breasts were bare, while her skirts were turned up and her knickers torn, so that her genitals were exposed. Near the body a pair of pocket scissors were found. On a chair near the body lay a chopper. The throat of the murdered woman showed clear signs of strangulation.

'The bed was in disorder. There was a spot on the sheet, caused by vomiting, and the chamber under the bed also contained a discharge of this nature. There was no sign of a search having been made for money or valuables; nothing except a lady's watch was missed. According to the post-mortem carried out by the police surgeons, Frau H. died of strangulation and internal haemorrhage resulting from stab wounds in her heart and lung, while the older woman died of strangulation. Her genitals were also injured, apparently by scratching.

'*There was no certain evidence of sexual assault...*'*

Another important feature found in sadists is that which Dr Braun calls "aloofness", although one need not go all the way with him in regarding the present-day tendency towards dissociation from existing social and political environments as so potentially inflammable as he seems to regard it. Nevertheless, it is true that the sadist does attribute to himself the prerogatives of impunity and even godhead. He thinks he is untouchable because no one is worthy to oppose him. This is borne out by the imaginative ravings of de Sade, the monsters in whose stories always performed their atrocities beyond the reach of the law or because they were a law unto themselves. The same is true of Sacher-Masoch's sadists, whose fiendish rampaging went on until poetic justice in the form of *gendarmes* (or *pandours*) or the enraged peasantry caught up with them.

Another salient and interesting similarity concerns the two novelists' attitude to religion. Both made scathing references to Christianity, and de Sade was positively blasphemous. But, though God and God's representatives

* *Sexual Anomalies and Perversions*, Torch Publishing Co. Ltd. (Pp. 467-8).

15

made his blood boil (as he says in *Juliette*), he probably 'denies the divinity of God' because, as Braun puts it, '*he is God*'.* The words which Sacher-Masoch puts into the mouth of the bandit Mikulev in the story BAJKA (and which are evidently meant to be convincing, for the pious girl is almost won over by them) are less virulent than de Sade's anti-Catholic outpourings, but hardly less uncompromising. Everyone who hates and is resentful is to that extent given to cruelty, but the arch-sadist who destroys his victim completely, thus denying the sacredness of a fellow human being's life, in so doing denies God and sets himself up in the place of the Deity: he is anti-Christ in that he takes upon himself the right and the role of reversing and annihilating what Christ stands for.

The male sadist, then, performs sadistic acts against the world because he despises the world: he hates everyone but himself (though in fact he may hate himself worst of all, without realising it, for being different from others). It is this difference, which Brecht calls *Verfremdung* (estrangement) and Braun interprets as "alienation" or "aloofness", that makes him feel superior, when he is really abysmally inferior, mentally and possibly physically also.

The female masochist submits to sadistic acts against herself, because she despises herself and hates herself for being what she is. Her submission to suffering is a craving for atonement, for expiation, and thereby for salvation—though in the event, she rejects salvation (so long as her abnormal impulses control her), for if she is saved from herself she will no longer need to suffer and she has come to accept suffering as pleasurable in itself, as a sex-substitute—*i.e.* as something that provides what normal sex fails to afford her. (Human beings are capable of conditioning themselves to the most extraordinary situations, as every experienced clinician knows only too well.)

These facts suggest a clue to a point of comparison

* Dr Walter Braun: *The Cruel and the Meek*, Luxor Press Ltd.; 9/6. (P. 17).

between a male-female sadomasochistic relationship and a female-male one, which for so long has baffled researchers. If sadism is some form of sexual cruelty arising out of resentment, and masochism is a form of reflexive sadism, then we may look to find in the female sadist a resentment against something or other and in her male victim (in so far as he is submissive) a parallel resentment, which may be straightforward or inverted.

It is not difficult to see that the most common resentment in the female sadist is the sense of penis-deprivation, the sense of anger at not being equipped like a man. This condition is much more common than most people (especially women) are ready to believe. Its most frequent manifestations are to be found in "butch" (masculine-type) lesbianism and transvestitism (the urge to dress as a man). Many lesbians who play the active role in tribadic relationships make use of a false penis (godemiché or dildo) during the act, besides affecting masculine clothes and short hair. Hermaphroditism (possessing characteristics, physical and/or otherwise, of both sexes at once) and androgyny (possessing physical characteristics of the opposite sex) may give rise to more or less complicated urges to exchange roles, but relatively seldom, I think, occasion such resentments as erupt in sadistic acts. Nevertheless, fascinating situations are common enough. It may be of interest to the reader, in this connexion, to revert for a moment to the case of Frau N.L., with which I began this commentary. Stekel's notes contain these observations:

'She frequently dreams that she is a man, goes out in men's clothes, and has wished she could take part in a military campaign as a soldier.

'She is bisexual, with clearly defined homosexual tendencies, which, however, are now firmly suppressed. It is because she was determined to be a normal woman that she married her husband. The conflict with her own masculinity, which she seeks to prevent from expressing itself, accounts for the particular scenes she is constantly indulging in. She chastises a man and makes him long for her sexually but in vain: it is the man in herself whom she is punishing and depriving, to make him expire with yearning.

'Her sadism is apparently directed only against men. It is projected outwards from within. Basically she is sadistic towards her masculine component and masochistic as man. This means the woman in her is sadistic, because she has to suppress the man; the man in her derives pleasure from masochistic motives!'

Physical hermaphroditism is, fortunately, rare, and the direction of sexual impulses that results from it will probably depend, in the last analysis, upon physiological considerations that are too complicated to be discussed in this necessarily cursory examination. As for androgyny, I feel I can hardly do better than quote Hirschfeld's remarks in *Sexual Anomalies and Perversions*:—*

'Considering that there is hardly an otherwise normal person who does not bear at least indications of the opposite sex, that all men have nipples, that very many women have at least a downy growth on the upper lip, as well as on the arms and legs, it is easy to see that there must be many graduations between the man with feminine breasts and the bearded woman on the one hand, and the complete man and woman on the other. And the latter, though conceivable, are hardly ever encountered. Thus it is not correct to diagnose androgyny if a man looks somewhat "feminine" or if he has hardly any hair on his body and face. On the other hand, androgyny may be assumed if a man has feminine breasts, a feminine voice, and a feminine pelvis. In the same way, it is incorrect to diagnose androgyny in a woman merely because she has more hair than usual on her face and body, but correct to do so if the facial hair has the character of a regular beard or if the other physical characteristics tend towards masculinity.'

Clearly, however, neither hermaphroditism nor androgyny can provide us with anything like a wholly satisfactory scientific explanation for the kind of tyrannical female sadist and servile male masochist encountered in the tales

* *Op. cit.* (Pp. 170-1).

of Leopold von Sacher-Masoch,—nor, in spite of the preference of women like Sarolta (in THE HYENA) and Varvara (in VARVARA PACADIN) for masculine clothes, can we profitably ascribe their conduct to a mere taste for transvestitism. Sacher-Masoch's own explanation (as supplied in LOLA), in my view, will not suffice either. I believe the likeliest explanation for such women is to be found in what is sometimes called "penis-envy"—resentment, as I have said, at not being equipped like the male—and its concomitant compensation-mechanism of despising the male and feeling superior to him. Naturally, this penis-envy is seldom present to consciousness, but the very fact of its being latent and deviational makes it more sinister and potentially more explosive. And even if he had been aware of such implications, Sacher-Masoch, despite his strange tastes, was too much of a "Victorian" prude to make mention of them.

The case of Stekel's patient, Frau N. L. is certainly, as we have seen, a further example. These women are frequently frigid towards normal sexual intercourse, as Stekel's patient admitted she was. I myself was recently consulted by a good-looking woman of 26 who confessed that the only thing that gave her complete satisfaction was *cunnilinctus*. But her husband, though willing to satisfy her in this way, insisted on mutual oral stimulation by the *soixante-neuf* (69) method. She told me frankly that she hated to have to take her husband's organ into her mouth, although there was no question of uncleanliness as they invariably resorted to this form of mutual excitation only after bathing each other. She found herself feeling more and more resentful and "humiliated" as her own excitement became more intense, and was quite sure that there was a risk that "one of these days" she would do her husband a serious injury by biting his penis.

Apropos of this, Hirschfeld recalls an extraordinary incident:- 'A well-known "lady-killer" in Cairo who was importuning a Turkish girl, fell a victim to an act of sexual revenge devised by her father and brothers. The man was invited to the house and left alone with the girl, who

19

first excited him, then took his erected penis into her hand and bent it so violently that he sustained a fracture of the penis, and was thereby rendered harmless. The girl was sentenced to pay the man monetary compensation.' Hirschfeld adds a note that 'fracture of the penis in an erect state is possible, and consists in the bursting of the *corpora cavernosa*, or blood-vessels, which are filled with blood, by sudden violent bending.'*

In the tales in this book, at least four women (Lola, Bajka, Seraphita, and the Baroness von Gotha) are of this kind. Maruvka (in The Red Manor-House) and Varvara Pagadin make themselves available to their male partners, cynically, as a means to an end. On the other hand, Irma (in The Lady Who Tamed Lions) and the Countess Vlasta (in The Wild Huntress) hate insanely through monstrously selfish jealousy. Kaschanka (in The Athaliah Of Zlota Reka) and Sarolta (in The Hyena) are the outstanding examples of women whose resentment explodes when they are rejected by the men they desire (the "Hell-hath-no-fury-like-a-woman-scorned" theme).

The fallacy in Sacher-Masoch's life and work, and the real tragedy of it, is his mistaken belief that there are *so many* sadistic women. (That he himself did not distinguish "ordinary" cruelty from sexual cruelty was due to the prevailing ignorance, in his day, of any such distinction). That there are cruel women in the world, that their cruelties can be every whit as ruthless and implacable as men's, are facts only too well documented by history; but that a woman can be impelled to the most heinous acts of violence by a hidden resentment at being physically inferior to a man is something that Sacher-Masoch vaguely apprehended but very imperfectly understood—and indeed it may be doubted whether it is fully understood even today, by *anyone*. He was aware that such women have always existed, sought in history (which was his special subject—at 20 he was already a Lecturer in History at the University of Graz) for an explanation, thought he had found it, and seems to have deduced from this that cruel-

* *Sexual Anomalies and Perversions*: Pp. 387-8.

ty towards men is endemic in women. As Alexander Pope said: 'A little knowledge is a dangerous thing.'

Another significantly erroneous assumption of his comes about, it seems to me, because he is not aware of the operation of a sadomasochistic relationship in the guise of a sex-substitute (to which I have already made reference). He himself needed to be whipped by his woman partner dressed in furs, in order to be capable of performing the normal sex act and reaching a climax. In other words flagellation was to him a sex-stimulant, but did not supplant normal heterosexual intercourse entirely. No doubt, during this prelude of ill-treatment, in order to heighten the effect, aural as well as visual and physical stimulations were made use of. (We are told by one of his biographers that he even asked, on one occasion, to be beheaded, though evidently this diversion was too extreme to be taken seriously). It is one thing to make the most extravagant protestations orally, but quite another matter to carry them wholly into effect. This is not to say, however, that Sacher-Masoch did not invite—and receive—very substantial punishment,—and apparently, as the years went by, he needed more and more severe whippings to produce satisfactory results. But, even so, he lets his imagination run away with him a little too much at times in his fictional narratives. In THE HYENA, for example, Baron Steinfeld is suspended over a well-stoked fire until the agony of his roasted feet causes him to lose consciousness; then he has them mangled in the terrible Iron Boot, and has his fingers and thumbs crushed in thumb-screws. Yet, when Sarolta offers him herself at last, he staggers eagerly towards her to enjoy his reward, though he can take no more than a halting step before he crumples at her feet. Such sexual persistence in a jaded middle-aged man who a moment before has been at death's door and only with the utmost difficulty revived, seems to me, to say the least, improbable. I find the revenge of the young Polish revolutionary against Lola altogether more feasible.

We have seen, then, how we may account for female

sadism, as well as male-female sadomasochistic relationships. It remains to enquire what makes a man willing to
be a victim for a woman sadist. Clearly, again, androgyny
provides no reliable answer, for Sacher-Masoch is at pains,
in more than one story, to assure us that his servile masochists are manly men. Seraphita (in GIRLS WHO WHIP
MEN) stresses this point. (' . . . among the most determined,
the keenest adherents one finds, in particular, robust,
healthy young fellows, built like powerful wrestlers ready
for the fray, those handsome, blond, pink-cheeked officers
with square shoulders and chests bulging like bucklers,—
yes, heaps of officers, who could knock us down with the
merest flick of their fingers and yet who, looking forward
to this mystic martyrdom, can no longer bring themselves
to want any other kind of love . . . ') If the masculine
female-orientated servile masochist behaved as he does
because of resentment at being male, he presumably *would*
be a case of androgyny and therefore effeminate in his
make-up. There is no evidence that Sacher-Masoch himself was of this type (de Sade, incidentally, *was* effeminate-
looking); and he is insistent that his male characters were
not. The only explanation, then, would seem to be that
the resentment in these cases is, as I said earlier, reflexive,
or directed against the self. Clearly, the possible reasons
for such self-resentment are manifold, and virtually limit-
less. Nowadays, we are familiar with the condition. "Inferiority complex" has become a household expression, and
like many household expressions is frequently a misnomer.
Nevertheless, every servile masochist (*i.e.* every person
who submits without resistance to the situation of being
a slave, or who purposefully subjects himself to slavery)
is suffering, in some degree, from the conviction of inferiority. Sacher-Masoch's own life abounds with indications
that such was the case with him.

Fetishism is a further manifestation of this complex:
to regard some object or association as an indispensable
condition for procuring sexual satisfaction is evidently
to surrender to its influence and to that extent, at least,
to be dominated by it, *i.e.* to be inferior to it. In the case

of Sacher-Masoch the fetish was furs. One may argue that whips and other flagellating instruments, fetters, leather boots, and foot-licking were all fetishistic associations for him too. But one must distinguish, I think, between what I would call causative and consequential fetishes. Sacher-Masoch was evidently addicted to fur, as he says Lola was for example, and as a person might be oddly moved by a certain kind of perfume, or by some part of the body such as a woman's breasts or buttocks or legs. He was also, incidentally, inordinately fond of cats and loved to stroke them. (He strangled his favourite kitten, however, when, towards the end of his life, his sanity completely deserted him.) He seems therefore to have supposed that *everyone* delights in furs, and again arguing from the specific to the general, believed he had found the reason in an "atavistic trait"—because in pre-history human beings were covered with hair, were shaggy, he says, like wild animals! This argument confirmed, strengthened and thence perpetuated his addiction. More importantly, there is evidence to show that in his formative years he was chastised by a female relative for spying on her while she was being seduced by a lover; her husband surprised her in the act and she whipped him from the room indignantly and then wielded the same instrument on the unfortunate Leopold who, astonished by the amazing resourcefulness of the woman, was unable to avoid making a sound and giving himself away. Significantly, the unfaithful wife was wearing, as she habitually did, a fur-trimmed jacket (called a *kazabaika*).

Once in the grip of the association between imperious women wearing furs and inferior men being thrashed by them, it was an easy (not to say inevitable) step to admiration for high boots (a traditional association, this) and, ultimately, to foot-licking and other forms of symbolic prostration. Male servile masochism is fundamentally and essentially a surrender of all dignity, a complete abdication of personal sovereignty, a renunciation of the right to satisfy (or even to have) tastes or desires of one's own that do not serve the tastes and desires of the "Domina".

23

In view of this, the kissing and licking of feet are part of the regular programme of submissiveness.

If Sacher-Masoch had been less of a prude, less circumscribed by the ambivalent moral values of the society he lived in; if he had given his perversion absolutely free play, he would have performed *cunnilinctus* and *anilinctus* also—though even if he had done so, false modesty and the conventional tabus would have forbidden all mention of such practices.

Magnus Hirschfeld reminds us that masochism, even in its most degrading forms, is of incalculable antiquity, and that disgusting acts like *anilinctus* and coprolagnia (deriving gratification from seeing or thinking of faeces) feature in the folklore of most peoples: practically every language has some expression comparable to 'Kiss my arse!', etc. Faeces are not associated only with masochism, though their use in sadistic acts is probably a further confirmation of the inseparability of sadistic and masochistic associations. Hirschfeld records an amazing case—that of the nuns of the Notre Dame de Charité at Tours, France,—which achieved notoriety in the French press in 1902:-

'The punishments thought out by the nuns were of a medieval character. For instance, sometimes the girls had to kiss the feet of their school mates or do "tongue crosses"; which means that the girl guilty of some trifling transgression had to prostrate herself before the holy sister and draw crosses on the ground with her tongue. This was done in the refectory, in the kitchen, and sometimes even in the lavatory. If a girl became sick in the process, the lavatory duster was stuffed into her mouth. The strait jacket was worn by girls not for hours but for days at a time. Girls sentenced to such punishment had to eat from earthenware pots, with their heads pushed into the pot. One particularly holy sister who rejoiced in the euphonious name, Marie Sainte-Rose du Cœur de Jésus, sometimes smeared the faces of her victims with mud and even stuffed her own excreta into their mouths. The so-called "water-trial" consisted in holding the head of a child wearing a strait jacket down in a basin of water until its throat rattled. The severest punishment was confinement in the "death chamber", a damp cellar in which the dead of the convent used to lie in state.'*

Fellatio, says Hirschfeld, 'is very frequently practised as a desirable act by women in sexual bondage.' Some of these women feel, at times, an overmastering desire to swallow the male semen. *Cunnilinctus* is a typical preference among male masochists. 'Whereas the sexually *normal* person may sometimes indulge in this act, in order to induce excitement in the beloved woman, thereby, in a sense, doing her a *favour*, a favour which indirectly increases his own pleasure, in the case of the masochist it is always an act of self-abasement. To him *cunnilinctus* symbolises complete dog-like devotion and submission. There is, in addition, the association of ideas arising from the position of the excretive organs, *i.e.*, the organs which perform the "lowest animal functions".'†

There is almost no limit to the variety of manifestations, even to the most improbable, in which masochism, male and female, seeks an outlet. Jealousy itself, in the opinion of some researchers, is a form of masochism, at any rate when it is deliberately fostered to an excessive degree. We have already dealt at some length with servile masochism, in which the subject desires to be treated as a slave. There is also puerile masochism in which the subject wishes to be treated as a child; zoomimic masochism in which he assumes the identity of an animal; impersonal masochism in which the subject is content to be an inanimate object, such as a footstool on which the "stern mistress" may rest her feet, or a mat or rug for her to wipe her feet on. And within these categories there are subdivisions, such as transvestite masochism, in which a man insists on dressing as a young girl and in being treated as such; and so on.

One of the most commonplace of all forms is verbal masochism, in which a man or a woman likes to be in-

* *Sexual Anomalies and Perversions*, Pp. 374-5.
† *Op. cit.*

sulted or addressed in obscene terms, and particularly to have the most intimate parts of the body referred to in the most vulgar manner. A woman of 22 confessed to me not long ago that she loved her man friend to pretend to rape her, and even put up quite a struggle to compel him "to fight for it": he had to tear her clothes and pinch and pull the *labia* of her vagina, and to refer to the act as he was about to perform by a word she normally heartily disliked and regarded as 'filthy'. Stekel records the case of a Mrs Y. whose masochistic libido impelled her to seek as a partner a heterosexual woman who was willing to assume the corresponding "counter-role". Her impulse was to procure for her partner 'an orgasm at any price.' Y. was subjected to verbal insults of the lowest sort, was beaten, trampled upon, scratched, pricked; licked the feet, vulva, anus of the friend, offered her mouth to be urinated into, and so on, and then was present when intercourse took place. She was subjected to a very severe sentence because the Penal Code paragraph dealing with her offences took a grave view of her peculiar predilections. Y., Stekel tells us, remained completely frigid in ordinary heterosexual intercourse in which she herself was a partner, unless she was roughly treated at the same time, pricked, insulted, or spat upon.

These, of course, are extreme cases, and clearly pathological. The fact remains, however, that pain and pleasure are so intimately bound up in sensual behaviour that few normal men and women do not, at times at least and for the sake of heightening sensation by the introduction of variety, enjoy the infliction or submission to minor acts of violence.* From the lover's pinch or bite that barely leaves a bruise or raises a blood blister to the unimaginable atrocities of sadistic murderers or the female tyrants of Sacher-Masoch's stories there is an infinite gradation, not only of action but also of motivation. Yet, fundamentally, when all is said and done, the same elements are at work, and normalcy is only a matter of a salutary balance

* Some very interesting examples of this sort of thing are given in my book *Secret Techniques of Erotic Delight* (Luxor Press 9/6), Chapter 12.

and control; truly, when we see or hear of some sadistic monster who has committed a quite irrational atrocity, we may say to ourselves: 'There but for the grace of God go I!'

Today, in the late "sixties," we are witnessing a variety of campaigns to neutralise and correct the current trend to violence. We hear of "Love-ins" and of "Flower Power" and of such slogans as "Make Love, not War!"

Unfortunately, these movements can achieve nothing, because they are founded on fallacy—the common fallacy of equilibrating love and hate as equal and opposite forces. They are nothing of the kind. Though in a certain sense they may be opposites, they are by no means equal. Hate is not only infinitely older than love; it is infinitely more powerful.

The absence of love is not hate: it may be indifference or apathy or a simple disposition to take an existing situation for granted. The savage who hates anyone that insults, attacks or endangers his tribe (and turns the full force of his resentment upon the offender) does not *ipso facto* and correspondingly *love* anyone that respects, defends or protects it. He simply takes him for granted and lives in peace with him. Love is a sublimation and a much more refined development than anything known to savagery. It is primarily an emotional condition. Hate is an impulse, an instinct, and man reacts to instinct like any other animal, blindly, automatically, impetuously. It is only with the advent of what is properly called civilisation that our primeval instincts are apprehended, analysed and brought under rational restraint. Affection is one of the "finer feelings" that come with the dawning of civilisation: affection is a synthesis of approbation, and love is the idealisation of affection. Tenderness is the sublimation of love.

On the other hand, hate is the crystallisation of resentment. Anger is explosive hate. Cruelty is the blast when hate explodes. These are positive, compulsive forces. Affection, love, tenderness are benign emotive states. Of

27

themselves these emotions can accomplish nothing—nothing, that is, that affects our fellow men or the world at large, so long as the rest are resentful and determined to resist. They are ideals or norms. And ideals can have no conquering power over brute force.

Occasionally, but relatively rarely, love too may erupt in violence, but when it does it cannot, in the nature of things, be a violence directed against the outside world, even though the outside world is the source of the trouble. Love will destroy *itself*, take its own life, rather than convert itself into the hate that is necessary to make retributive violence effective. This is why the broken-hearted lover takes his own life. This is what accounts for the suicide pact of the Romeo-and-Juliet type of "star-crossed lovers."

The only thing that can save a world like ours that is so racked with hate and violence is the inculcation of tolerance; that alone can draw the teeth of our manifold resentments.

Considering that the lust for inflicting pain and the victims' powerless resignation to it are probably as old as man himself, it is remarkable that only for the past eighty years or so have there been words by which to refer to these phenomena. For thousands of years, that is to say, sadism and masochism must either have been taken for granted or (their sexual undertones being unperceived) passed for straightforward manifestations of cruelty and submissiveness. It is psychoanalysts, sexual physiologists and sexologists, like Freud, Jung, Moll, Bloch, Féré, Krafft-Ebing, Havelock Ellis, Stekel, Hirschfeld, and so on, who recognised and highlighted the sex mechanisms at work, though to be sure there is far from uniformity of opinion about the precise workings. Krafft-Ebing, through his monumental *Psychopathia Sexualis*, familiarised the world with the terms sadism and masochism, and thereby sadomasochism; it was Schrenk-Notzing who coined the neologism "algolagnia" to express the perplexing sado-masochistic pleasure-through-pain complex. Sadism and masochism and their corollaries are, by definition, sexual in orientation. How far basic cruelty and acceptance of it are sexually motivated it is difficult and perhaps impossible to say: clearly generalisations are in any case valueless.

It is also debatable whether the Marquis de Sade and the Chevalier Leopold von Sacher-Masoch really deserved to lend their names to the peculiar perversions which have been named after them. It is certain that those perversions were not invented by them; it is dubious whether these men were even very satisfactory protagonists. There is no evidence that de Sade, in his personal life, did more than disturb the surface of the cesspool of enormities he describes in his works. Sacher-Masoch, on the other hand, was much more conditioned in his own conduct by a compulsive desire to induce his women to make him suffer than are the male characters in most of the stories he wrote. In the majority of the ten stories in this book, for instance, it is not the men who are determined to suffer but the women who are determined to make them. In two of the tales (LOLA and GIRLS WHO WHIP MEN) Sacher-Masoch puts into the words of male characters an aversion to feminine acts of violence. In LOLA, writing in the first person he affects to be expressing his own point of view when he says: 'I kept clear of her, and took care to make sure that my meetings with her were few and far between.' In other words, these are essentially (in the main) stories about sadistic women rather than about masochistic men. Indeed, a number of the stories are taken from a series published under the general title of *Grausame Frauen* (Cruel Women); and I must say it has always seemed to me that this was Sacher-Masoch's chief obsession—the cruelty of women, whether for sexual or asexual reasons, whereas the true masochist is obsessed by his or her own desire for suffering and is only indirectly concerned with the attitude of the person who inflicts the suffering. I believe it is important that this should be made clear, as there is a very widespread but glib assumption that Sacher-Masoch was the representative *par excellence* of the aberration that has been coined from his name. That he was among the first to express in his writings the idea that suffering could be enjoyable and sexually stimulating, and, above all, what the vast majority of his contemporaries rejected as totally inconceivable—that a man could be eager and willing to suffer at the hands of a woman—is a different matter altogether.

His persistent theory—that women are by nature more cruel than men—which he repeated *ad nauseam* in his writings and sought so desperately to prove in his private life, was not very satisfactorily borne out by his own experiences: he had the very devil of a job to persuade his various women to be as cruel to him as he wanted them to be. At the same time, his literary talents, which were by no means inconsiderable, were debased and adulterated by his unrelenting reiteration of this favourite theme. When the literary critics drew attention to this, he blamed his wife and told her accusingly that if she would wear furs and whip him soundly more often he would not need to invent such women all the time.* In other words, his writings provided an escape—not *from* something, but *to* that which he longed for: they provided him with a means of obtaining a vicarious satisfaction by appearing to confirm that the world really does abound with female monsters who scorn man's virility and make him grovel in the dust for the privilege of being kicked and beaten and treated as a slave.

The truth, I think, purged of all wishful thinking and misguided idealism, is that cruelty is a common human vice expressing itself in the most diverse and diabolical forms in the actions of both women and men. Practised by either sex, there are virtually no limits to the enormities it may give rise to.

In LOLA, appropriately enough the first story in this book, Sacher-Masoch outlines his theory, which purports to prove that women's contemptuous rejection of men as

* This and other salient features in the private life of Sacher-Masoch are much more fully dealt with in Dr Walter Braun's *The Cruel and the Meek*, Luxor Press; 9/6. (Pp. 99-117).

the stronger sex is a deeply-rooted, subconscious, atavistic trait the origins of which are shrouded in pre-history. But his arguments are not altogether convincing and do not square with what we know today, although it is perhaps remarkable that he considered it incumbent upon him to produce arguments at all, in support of an order of things that he claimed was so natural and common. He mentions that 'in all nature' the female first resists the advances of the male and only succumbs after a struggle. He does not, however, make clear why the re-emergence of this instinct as a throwback should make a woman want to *destroy* a man as ruthlessly as his own "heroines" get rid of their male victims.

The desire to be raped, which is common enough, and the survival of the impulse to struggle against seduction by the male, are wholly credible manifestations of the trait to which Sacher-Masoch refers, but I see no reason why, because of it, women should yearn to obliterate the male entirely. There may be a seeking for revenge*, but not an urge for annihilation,—except where other factors supervene which are unrelated to the primeval relic Sacher-Masoch makes so much of.

Again, he makes the point that there are species of insects in which the female maims or destroys the male after he has fertilised her. But the life of many insects is ephemeral anyway and hardly comparable with that of human beings; the male may well have no reason to go on living after he has made it possible for many of his kind to succeed him; and it would be singularly short-sighted of Nature if she were to let it be the female who is destroyed by the male after mating and before her reproduction processes have been completed. There are, too, species (as Sacher-Masoch himself mentions) in which the female's life comes to an end with the accomplishment of procreation. Obviously, these are devices employed by Nature to ensure that the numbers of such creatures shall be restricted within manageable limits; and if there were any reason to suppose that at some point in the chain

* *Op. cit.:* Pp. 79-80.

of evolution similar genetic peculiarities manifested themselves in human beings, the only vestige of them one might expect to encounter would be in relation to parturition. But not even Sacher-Masoch pretends that any of his vicious females tortures, maims or kills her males because she is impelled to this course by the mystical stirrings of some procreative force deep in her being; as a matter of fact, some of them (like Lola, Bajka, the Countess Vlasta in THE WILD HUNTRESS, and Maruvka in THE RED MANOR-HOUSE) are not even directly interested in having sexual intercourse with the men they persecute . . . Clearly, then,—or so it seems to me—we must look elsewhere than in the sex life of bees and spiders for an explanation of woman's inhumanity to man.

Although cruelty and submission to it are, as I suggested at the very beginning of this Preamble, of incalculable antiquity, there is no reason to suppose that sex originally entered into the question at all. It is because (ever since the revelations of Freudian psychoanalysts and sex researchers in general) we have become conditioned in the twentieth century to think every human proclivity is somehow related to a sexual urge that it is such a commonplace fallacy to imagine that cruelty *must* be somehow sexually motivated, and to confuse all cruelty with sadism and too much of humility and forbearance with masochism. I do not believe that an ill-tempered boor, or a drunken lout, who throws his weight about and bullies physically weaker people around him is *ipso facto* a sadist who derives sensual pleasure or sexual stimulation from his callous actions. A man who flogs a tired horse, thrashes a child, or kicks a dog, is cruel, but not necessarily a sexual maniac or pervert. It is when cruelty becomes associated in some way with sexual lust, whether blatantly or not, that sexual abnormality creeps in.

Primitive peoples are cruel (by "civilised" standards) but they are not sadistic. Even less, perhaps, are they masochistic. This is because they are not sexually inhibited as are those whose religions have persisted in branding sex as evil and thereby created deviations to bypass sin. The wild man of Borneo the glans of whose penis has been perforated in his youth and who, when he has carnal contact with his woman, wears through the hole a metal rod surmounted at both ends by balls and spikes—the murderous ampallang which would lacerate the tender insides of any Western woman whose vaginal orifice had to suffer its intrusion—is no sadist: he is simply prepared to do his duty as a virile seducer whose partner would despise him if he were less formidably equipped. He is no masochist either: he has borne the martyrdom of mutilation because it is his manly duty to do so—just as a so-called civilised man will shave his face meticulously or a woman undergo the torments of the beauty parlour to render themselves more pleasing to each other in bed. Other, even more barbarous, customs—such as male subincision and female circumcision—, cruelly inhuman as they seem to us, are not manifestations of sadism but are dictated by sincere, however mistaken, muddled notions of hygiene and propriety. So, too, chastity belts, seraglios guarded by eunuchs, and convents and monasteries, are outward manifestations by people who think themselves infinitely superior to Hottentots or Australian aborigines of a fervent intention to eschew evil and aspire to godliness. After all, the Chinese, who have always been remarkably free from sexual inhibitions, distrust and despise deliberate celibacy, particularly of women, as an attempt to usurpation of unnatural powers—and this is one of the reasons why nuns and priests have often been assaulted and massacred in China.

What I am trying to say is that sadism and masochism are pre-eminently products of *civilisation*, and, in particular, of the Judao-Christian religion—for these influences have, by banning sex and driving it into concealment, created an atmosphere in which the fundamental essence of human cruelty and bestiality is turned putrid and diseased by instincts that are too strong to submerge and too insistent to be denied. We no longer empty chamber-pots into the street from our bedroom windows or sit side by side on long communal lavatory seats to relieve our necessities; most of us do not spit on the floor; we do not provide entertainment by hanging and torturing people in public; we do not (in this country anyway) slaughter animals for meat by slitting their throats and hanging them up to die slowly from loss of blood. We regard these things as uncivilised and therefore tabu. But many people in the United States of America gang together and put on silly hoods and long white gowns in order to crucify Negroes with impunity: they lash them with wire whips or cut off their genitals with razor blades because they disapprove of the colour of their skins. And in war-time the best of us torture prisoners and strike down non-combatants with the most hideous weapons that our civilised scientists can devise. Let no one suppose, then, that fundamentally we are not as cruel as in the olden days, just because our methods are more sophistic-ated or because our views about what is publicly permiss-ible have undergone some modification. Man is basically an animal and animals can be fiendishly cruel to each other. But man has complicated his cruelty by infusing sex ingredients into it in a way that other animals have never learned to do. Good for them!

It was religion, too, that did much to foster torture. A priesthood élite that allots to itself the power and the right to interpret the Will of God readily sees fit to punish and to chasten those who it claims are guilty of heresy,—that is, of disconformity with its interpretations and disobedience to its dictates—and therefore in danger of losing their immortal souls. Since God is revealed as a jealous deity who will punish with everlasting suffering any who reject him, a timely spate of torturing on earth may bring the sinner to his senses and cause him to repent and thereby insure for himself eternal bliss; if repentance does not come in time, then a particularly painful death may be regarded by God as having discharged the debt in full and so obviate perpetual suffering in the hereafter. The same kind of argument lay behind the disciplines of fasting and flagellation and other forms of mortification

34

for relatively minor misdemeanours. The body must be denied or ill-treated or destroyed in order that the spirit may be safeguarded, purified and uplifted. The followers of Mohammed slaughtered Christians, the believers in Christ waged holy wars against the infidels of Islam; Catholics martyred Protestants, and Protestants wiped out Catholics with no less zealous thoroughness; in a few hundred years, until late in the past century, literally millions of women were burnt alive or otherwise put to death as witches, accused of trafficking with the Devil in one way or another, mainly in various forms of sexual misconduct. By now, you see, sex had come into its own and given its full, filthy, lecherous, sadistic colouration to sin. And the worst of it was that to so many people all over the world it all seemed so reasonable. Was it not woman who spoilt everything in the first place by seducing man in the Garden of Eden?—and here she was again still at her old tricks, even seducing the Devil himself this time, who no longer found it convenient to disguise himself as a serpent.

Once the principle of defining sin is admitted and the right to identify it and punish it is conceded, there is no stopping the sin-seekers and little protection for the sinners. And when once you accord to certain members of the community the right to take the lives of other members, thereby denying the sacredness of life itself and the inviolability of the individual whose life is taken, then, it seems to me, it is no longer possible to control the extent or the magnitude of punishment. In the days when a man was hanged for stealing a loaf of bread, although no worse fate would overtake him if he chose to murder his wife instead, it was clearly not enough merely to hang him if he insulted the King, for while it might not matter if the value of his wife's life was equated with the value of a loaf of bread, it would clearly be monstrous not to make it evident what a gulf of difference yawned between petty pilfering and lese-majesty. So in the case of treason the culprit could expect to be drawn and quartered as well. Of course, the drawing and quartering did not really make up for the relative heinousness of the offence, but there was necessarily a limit to what could be done: when a man had been hanged, taken down before he had quite expired, had his entrails torn out, and then been cut into four pieces, he was well and truly dead and there was little point in pursuing the penalty any further. Even so, Robert François Damiens, the French would-be regicide, who didn't even succeed in his half-hearted attempt on the life of Louis XV, was subjected to what has generally been regarded as one of the most hideous and protracted punishments ever meted out to a felon in modern times.* The fact remains, however, that if he had been a less powerfully built man his sufferings would have been over much sooner.

It is true in general terms, I think, that in the last analysis it is probably impossible—and certainly arbitrary— to separate the *right* to take life from the *manner* of inflicting death. This seems to be borne out by the wide variety of ways in which "judicial" executions are carried out in the different places where capital punishment still obtains—hanging, garrotting, the gas chamber, the electric chair, the guillotine, and so on.

The awful thing is that the right to take life has gone on so long unquestioned, not only by those who have claimed it but by those who have been threatened by it. In the feudal societies of places to which Sacher-Masoch refers in these stories—and the feudalism had continued at least up to the days of his own boyhood—the lord of the manor literally had the power of life and death over his vassals. If he could take their life, he could do what he liked to them in other respects—and frequently did. Stories like THE RED MANOR-HOUSE and THE WILD HUNTRESS are not, therefore, in their settings at least, exaggerations. Nor, for that matter, are some of the cruelties described. Just as de Sade wrote of things that, horrible though they are to read about, were actually perpetrated in pre-Revolution France, so, too, the crucifying of people

* The story of the execution of Damiens is told a little more fully in Dr Braun's *The Cruel and the Meek*, Luxor Press; 9/6. (P. 83).

to barn doors, lashing them with flails, and fixing them over ant-hills and leaving them to be gnawed to death, were methods of execution with which young Leopold had become familiar by the time he was ten. Even the story of Sarolta's bathing in warm human blood to restore her youth and beauty (in THE HYENA) is not an original idea: women of antiquity (and later), we are assured, made use of such blood-baths. Not all such atrocities were committed by the rich and powerful, however: some of the worst of them were the work of robbers and outlaws, and of the peasantry who, in 1846 when their tyrannical Polish masters rebelled against the local authorities, took advantage of the confused situation to turn what weapons they could muster against their own overlords.

In feudal times in our own country, as well as in most of the rest of Europe, the lord controlled the destinies of his serfs with unchallenged absolutism, though this is not to say that such power was not used beneficently, for undoubtedly it often was in many ways and in many individual cases; besides, it is difficult to imagine what alternative system could have been half so workable, given the complexities of the social and political life of the times. Nevertheless, abuses abounded too: this would inevitably follow from the failure to recognise the inviolable dignity of the individual. If a man could be seized and held in chains without trial, the person and honour of his wife and daughter might not be sacred either. There is no doubt that for centuries *jus primae noctis** prevailed— the feudal lord's right to have the first intercourse on her wedding-night with any girl among his serfs before handing her over to her husband. Social historians sometimes aver that this right was seldom observed; but while it is perfectly probable that in the case of an unwashed, unwholesome wench the lord might readily waive his privilege, it is asking too much of credulity, knowing what we do of man's cupidity, to suppose that many an ageing lecher would willingly forgo a legitimate opportunity to

* In some rural parts of Mexico, even to this day, the local priest reserves to himself the right to deflower virgin brides.

enjoy a pretty and submissive poppet who took pride in her appearance. Although Sacher-Masoch in his short stories makes no mention of this interesting custom, he does, in THE RED MANOR-HOUSE, make it clear that if a rich Lothario took a fancy to a bonny girl on his estates there was not much anyone could do to prevent his having his way with her. And if Maruvka's attitude is anything to go by, the girl herself might be the least likely to protest.

It is easy to see, then, that ultimately the forces we have been considering and that are the subject of the stories in this book, are forces that derive from social distinctions. Revolts and revolutions arise from resentment, and resentment, as we have said, gives rise to hate, and hate to cruelty. When cruelty becomes associated with sex (and sooner or later that is bound to happen), it becomes sadism, and sadism is inseparable from masochism, because sadomasochism, or algolagnia (which Hirschfeld defines as "pain-craving") is a bi-polar phenomenon in which the masochist is at the same time a sadist.

By "social distinctions" I mean the monstrous social inequalities that punctuate the pages of history and that go hand in hand with exaggerated and disproportionate authoritarianism. Slavery provides a useful case in point. Yet there is all the difference in the world between the benevolent slavery of Athens and the iniquitous plantation slaveries of the West Indies and the southern United States of America. One cannot have any doubt but that there were countless exceptions in both ages: there were maleficent slave-owners in ancient Greece and beneficent ones in Alabama, etc. Social distinction, even when it permits slavery, is not necessarily in itself evil: it is deplorable only because it opens the door to abuses—to resentment (on either side), to hatred, to anger, to cruelty, and incidentally to sadomasochistic states of mind and conduct. And the iniquity is not confined to one side more than to the other. When resentment erupts in angry cruelty, it is blind and indiscriminate. Hence lynchings and mob violence. Hence injuries to innocent bystanders when police get out of hand. The only thing that prevents a resentful slave from flogging his master and raping his master's daughters is his powerlessness; place weapons in his hands and open his master's doors to him and he will run amuck, loot, kill, rape and burn until his lust for revenge is sated. This has been demonstrated over and over again throughout history, from Spartacus' gladiatorial revolt to the Negro persecutions of the white settlers in the Belgian Congo. And it is the dread of such acts of revenge that makes the threat of Black Power so frightening to the white bigots who cringe behind Apartheid and the Ku Klux Klan.

This is the great evil of our times still. Perhaps it will always be so. Today it is youth, primarily, who are resentful—resentful of their elders' mismanagement and ineptitude; resentful of being sent to commit atrocities and die in wars that are not of their choosing and in which they do not believe; resentful of ethnical and social distinctions; resentful of discriminations between the sexes in an age of vaunted sex equality; resentful of being taught the wrong things by the wrong people in the wrong way in overcrowded schools. That they themselves may not be equipped, mentally and physically, to provide a satisfactory solution for these deficiencies is not the point: it only begs the question by admitting that a solution must still be found. But meanwhile the immediate effects of their resentment are there for all to see—in ripped-up streets, smouldering buildings, blazing motor-cars and busy hospitals. That these extremities bring discredit on their cause, arousing in non-demonstrative sectors of the population, a new resentment, is an exacerbation. Already one hears and reads in the newspapers of threats and demands for a "tougher line". Violence breeds violence, cruelty creates fresh enormities.

If there is a little less risk in our own day and age, however high feelings run, of resentment, anger and violence expressing themselves in sadomasochistic extremes, this is because concurrently with mounting resentment there has been a relaxation of sexual inhibition. The same young people who explode with social resentments have already

39

found outlets for their sexual desires. If they want to be promiscuous they can; if they prefer to behave like homosexuals the law no longer denies them that right; with substantial easing of censorship, if they are content to read about sex there is plenty for them to feast their eyes upon; and they can masturbate to their hearts' content without the bogeymen of grandfather's day threatening them with the asylum or an early grave.

God help us all if the authorities who strive to deny their social and political aspirations should be misguided enough to attempt to clamp down again upon their *libido sexualis* at the same time! The fate of Kiev's Police Chief Halikov* would be a merciful release compared with what might be cooked up for them by well-fed, sex-starved revolutionaries!

* See VARVARA PAGADIN.

LOLA

There is a type of woman who, ever since my boyhood, has invariably attracted me.

She is the woman with the eyes of a sphinx, whom desire makes cruel and cruelty makes desirous.

She is the woman with the body of a tigress, worshipped by man, although she in return torments and humiliates him. Whether, clad in a Biblical robe, she shares the couch of Holofernes; or, wearing a gleaming breastplate, she watches her lover broken on the wheel; or, adorned with the ermine cloak of a Sultana, she has her suitor hurled into the waters of the Bosphorus, this woman is always—uniquely herself.

The first time I met her, Lola struck me as a most agreeable companion.

Her father, a high-ranking officer in Lemberg, was a friend of my family. We were both still children when she first filled me with terror. It was in the garden where we had made for ourselves a house of leaves and intertwined branches. She had just left me, to go and sit on a bench some distance away. Thinking she was deeply engrossed in a day-dream, I went up to her in stealthy silence, intending to surprise her, to take her in my arms and give her a kiss. I was in love with her: that is to say I loved her as much as a boy of ten is capable of loving a little girl barely two years older.

I found her absorbed in tearing off the wings of half a dozen flies that were still alive, observing with rapt attention the little creatures' convulsions.

The expression on her face made me shudder.

It had something indescribable about it.

It evinced at the same time voluptuous pain, devilish joy, a grin that was awesome and horrible.

What was it then?

Anyway, I found her industry terrifying; and yet Lola fascinated me. I hated her, but at the same time she captivated my senses.

I was still a mere child when she was already a young lady, tall and good-looking; so she continued to treat me like a child: she went so far as to make me the confidant of her little secrets, of her passions, even of her vices.

Furs she loved to distraction, and she was possessed by an overmastering desire to persecute.

With her, cruelty was something innate, as with other women is preoccupation with their appearance, their clothes or with affairs of the heart.

I have hardly ever seen her when she was not dressed in a *kazabaika* lined and trimmed with fur.

One day, when we came back from a walk, she removed her cloak and took off her stays. After all, I was just a little boy: there was no need to bother about me. She then asked me to help her on with her *kazabaika* again.

As she stood there, folding her bare arms on her heavenly breasts, and she slipped into the soft fur, a voluptuous shiver convulsed her whole being. When I pressed a kiss on the nape of her neck, she cast an indescribable glance at me: a glance that I recognised immediately. It was precisely the expression of hers that I had observed once before,—that time when she was torturing those poor flies.

'When I am wrapped up in my furs, I feel like a big cat', she said to me one day, 'and I am seized by a devilish desire to play with a mouse; it must be a big mouse, though.'

At the same time, her eyes in the darkness took on a phosphorescent glow; and when one's hand stroked or smoothed her hair, it seemed as if a crackling of electric sparks came from it.

When Lola's figure was clothed in some sleek hide and

42

the delicious fur was caressing the rotundities of her breasts and hips, I felt overcome by an inexplicable charm.

At such times she irradiated the odour of a wild animal, and mingled with this, a suggestion of the most blood-thirsty lustfulness.

She thoroughly enjoyed situations in which she felt herself able to martyrise slaves, to subjugate men and ill-treat them. As we came away from a performance of *Essex* at the Opera House, she said to me: 'I would will-ingly give ten years of my life to be able to sign a death warrant and then to be present at the execution.'

In spite of all this, the girl was neither brutal nor ec-centric. On the contrary, she was in general rational and moderate, and even seemed to be as tender and refined in her make-up as she was sentimental. As she was not allowed to go into the barracks to watch the chastisement of soldiers punished with the bastinado or by being forced to run the gauntlet* Lola contrived to establish friendly relations with the wife of a warder who resided in the Prefecture of Police.

On this woman devolved the duty of applying corporal punishment to minors and to women, and she carried out this task without pity, but without savagery either, gravely and methodically, as though to her it were simply a question of fulfilling a joyless mission.

Nevertheless, to a much greater extent than the highly-strung Lola, she personified the cruel type of woman.

She was a young wench, strapping and powerful in build, with a purposive air; her cheeks glowed with the tints of freshness, her nose was snubly defiant, her mouth large, her lips thick, and her eyes cold and grey.

She dressed partly like a townswoman and partly like a woman of the country, and I could never resist following her with my eyes as she crossed the courtyard, with her short rustic sheepskin bodice undulating on her broad hips and a red foulard tied coquettishly at her neck.

Often when a flogging was in process Lola would slip

* This punishment consisted in making the delinquent pass along be-tween two rows of soldiers armed with birches.

into a corner, where she would remain huddled while the sentence was carried out, admiringly watching the warder's wife as, with her left hand resting on her hip, she wielded the birch. Lola seemed to be envious, wishing she could exercise this distressing function.

During the revolutionary troubles of 1846, a large number of schoolchildren were arrested for having taken part in the conspiracy. Among them was a high-school boy barely sixteen years of age who, according to the law, was too young yet to be sent to prison; he was, therefore, sentenced to receive thirty strokes of the birch.

Again Lola had the same strange desire to take upon herself the carrying out of the sentence.

She had no wish to have anything to do with the boys and girls punished for thefts or other ordinary misdeeds, but she immediately begged the jailer's wife to leave this adolescent revolutionary to her.

'Why not?' said the young woman, '—if the idea appeals to you.'

'Oh yes, it would give me the very greatest pleasure.'

'Well, all right, you shall have that pleasure then; but my husband must know nothing about it, neither he nor anyone else.'

The high-school boy, whose countenance already denoted manliness, would not willingly submit to a punishment he regarded as degrading. So he began to resist and flung himself at the feet of the jailer's wife as she, accompanied by two hefty women prisoners, approached him to tie his hands and feet.

'Don't beat me!' he begged, with tears in his eyes. 'Don't let me be dishonoured in such a shameful manner!'

'I am not going to beat you', replied the young woman, when she had sent her assistants away. 'But a beautiful lady has asked me to let her have an entirely free hand in this case, and *she's* going to do it.'

At first, the poor youth did not grasp her meaning, but when the jailer's wife picked him up in her arms and placed him on a bench, and Lola appeared, dressed in her *kazabaika*, her face covered with a black velvet mask, her sleeves rolled up, and holding a birch in her hand, he started to beg for mercy, but in vain.

Lola went up close to him and began to whip him.

Hands on hips, the jailer's wife was contemplating this spectacle with astonishment.

As the strokes became more and more violent and drew from the victim piteous yells of pain, Lola's companion burst into a laugh:

'Well, this is the first time', said she, 'that I have ever got such enjoyment out of it.'

Then, when Lola had finished, the jailer's wife in her turn administered to the schoolboy several more blows which she delivered with all her force.

'You say this has given you pleasure', commented Lola. 'As far as I'm concerned, that is putting it very mildly indeed. While I was whipping him I had such maddening sensations that I felt as if I would thrill to death!'

The town of Graz, nestling beside the delightful little river Mur, received its spiritual baptism from the King of Holland, the father of Napoleon III, who christened it *La Ville des Grâces sur les Bords de l'Amour*. It is the favourite retreat of retired Austrian officers and functionaries. It was there one day my father and Lola's, who was now a General, met again. And I too, after many years, saw once more the beautiful and strange girl of long ago.

She had grown taller and stronger, but her character had not changed. She still wore a *kazabaika* embellished with fur, and over her ottoman hung a whip.

'Are you still as cruel as in the old days?' I asked her.

'Do you want to find out?' she replied. 'If so, all you have to do is place yourself in my hands.'

I kept clear of her, and took care to make sure that my meetings with her were few and far between.

One morning in winter I saw her going by, unaccompanied, in an open sleigh; she recognised me and ordered the driver to stop, then called me over to her.

She raised her veil. She was pale and there was a disquieting fieriness in her gaze.

'Do you know where I have just come from?' she asked.

'It would be rather difficult for me to guess!'

'Well, I have been watching the execution of the assassin Baron Jomini!'

'You are joking, Lola!' I replied, stupefied.

'Not at all. Really! I assure you I was there; my nerves are still tingling with the indescribable thrill of that spectacle.'

As she uttered these words, a shiver ran through her as though from the biting cold, and she drew her fur closer round her.

'But didn't you feel the slightest pity?' I went on.

'There was only one thing I regretted.'

'What was that?'

'Not having the right to strike the fatal blow myself.'

'And would you then have spared his life?'

'By no means! I should have thought to myself that he was about to die on my orders and the thrill would have been much greater.'

'Lola!' I exclaimed. 'You're crazy.'

'I am certainly not, my friend. If I were to see that my passions made me odious to men, I would keep them to myself; but I know perfectly well that by being open and frank about them I succeed in enchaining men's hearts much more firmly than other women, for all their sentimental ogling. A woman who torments men will always be idolized. And, what is more, furs provide an additional stimulant.'

On this last point, Lola was quite right. At that moment, enveloped in her heavy, comfortable cloak, she looked to me like some superb wild animal; and involuntarily my hand stroked the fur and I felt as if I were caressing the coat of a beautiful tigress.

Some months later, I learnt that Lola had married a Major in the Lancers and had gone with her husband to Hungary, where his regiment was billeted in several villages and townships. The young couple resided at Prince Batyani's castle, the owner of which was only too pleased to place it at their disposal. It was winter again, and Lola was feeling bored to death. Then destiny provided her with a fatal plaything. One evening, Lola heard it mentioned as a topic of conversation among the officers that a young Pole, who had become involved in politics, had (such being so often the case in Austria) been conscripted into her husband's regiment as a private. She forthwith asked her husband to have the young man attached to their household staff.

'What for?' enquired her husband. 'If you have any idea about making life easier for him, forget it: it's nothing but a romantic dream. A traitor deserves no pity.'

'Quite the contrary', said Lola softly. 'I myself will punish him for his treachery.'

Using all her influence, she managed to get her own way. The Pole was taken on at the castle as a servant, at Lola's behest.

After that, she was no longer bored. To her it was devilishly exciting to humiliate the young man, who came from a good family, to persecute him and to torment him unmercifully. To all this he submitted uncomplainingly; indeed, it even seemed as if he endured with a certain eagerness the harassments that his master's wife inflicted upon him. Lola did not fail to notice this. One day, when she returned home from an outing on horseback and had just thrown off her *kazabaika*, she ordered the young Pole to pull off her boots and put on her little silken slippers for her. As he was kneeling before her to perform this by no means unpleasant duty, the poor fellow could not resist the temptation to raise her dainty foot and press his lips to it. She, however, pushed him abruptly away. Then she had him taken into the courtyard and watched with evident pleasure from her window the punishment with the bastinado that was meted out to him at her command.

From that moment onward, the fate of these two beings

47

was sealed. Some days afterwards, the Major had to leave his wife to undertake a tour of inspection.

He returned to find the bedroom doors locked. When he had forced his way in, he found the young man and Lola in bed together locked in each other's arms. Both were dead.

A few lines in the handwriting of the ill-fated Pole provided the necessary explanation. He had loved Lola, he confessed, and, to be avenged on her for her heartless treatment of him, he had raped and murdered her, and then taken his own life.

Such was the end of this cruel woman. Since that time, I have more than once come across women of her type, for the Eastern regions seem the natural habitat of these magnificent tigresses in velvet and furs, and I have come to know more and more about the mystical and terrifying problem of their voluptuous cruelty.

The salient characteristics of this heartless species, with all the magic power they exercise over the male, seem to me to be nothing less than an atavistic manifestation. Nature has, in creating these beings, endowed them with an instinctive recollection of a primeval urge. Throughout all Nature, the female at first resists the sexual advances of the male. Undoubtedly, man too, in bygone times, was subject to the same natural laws.

Consequently, every conquest was preceded by a struggle, and so it is that, even today, woman feels instinctively impelled to resist and dominate man.

As a result, woman's ill-treatment of man re-creates in him the illusion of true femininity.

It is always so.

As for fur, it too evokes the influence of pre-history, when human beings were covered with hair; and it conjures up a sensation of wild and bestial strength, which modern man in his feebleness finds utterly intoxicating.

The relationship between cruelty and lust, then, is assuredly an atavistic trait. The queen bee kills the male after the mating. Similarly, legend tells us that the Amazons of Scythia treated their menfolk as slaves and, when sated with sexual intercourse, cynically put them to death.

Another example: there are creatures whose own life comes to an end with the act of procreation. In the same way, with human beings, at the moment of fulfilment in their love-making, there is, as it were, a coalescence of the two extremes—life and death.

How often do lovers in the throes of their orgasm murmur: 'Let's die together'!

Nothing comes easier or more naturally to lovers than mutual suicide.

It was this same reminiscence that was at work in the mystic fertility ceremonies of Eleusis celebrating the birth of a new life, and that gave rise to the mad desire to torture, to mutilate, to kill, and to be tortured and killed.

It is this, too, that explains why the soldier, who is at all times ready to accept death as well as to give it, is such a firm favourite with women.

BAJKA

The Rumanian province at the foot of the Carpathians, where the mountains form the boundary between Bukovina and Moldavia, had for some days been in a state of unprecedented turmoil. Mikulev, the notorious robber chief, feared by the rich and deified by the common people, had raided the nunnery of Gumora by night and plundered it. He and his men had carried off everything that was removable,—money, securities and documents, as well as all the ancient treasure and the sacred vessels. For ten years the government had been searching for him, but without success, for the whole of the peasantry were on his side and, unsolicited, whenever necessary kept a look-out on his behalf or got a warning to him somehow. More than once he had waged open warfare on the soldiery and sent them home with bleeding heads.

On this occasion, also, the Abbess of the convent of Gumora had called in the help of the authorities, but in vain. No clue could they uncover to help them trace either the thieves or the booty. One evening, just as the Abbess was bewailing her misfortune to the *boyar** Voinescu, the protector of the nunnery, a peasant girl from one of the nearby mountain villages asked to be admitted to her presence.

'Perhaps she brings us news of the robbers', said the Abbess. 'Let her come in.'

The young woman who now entered, in her long, copiously-embroidered chemise, over which she wore nothing but a short sheepskin jacket, and with her proud, nobly-chiselled features, dark eyes full of fire and energy, her

* *Boyar(d):* in Russia and Rumania, a member of the privileged classes, a landowner and aristocrat.

superb build and her plump bosom, looked more like an empress that had arisen out of some Roman tomb than a homely peasant woman of the Carpathian mountain district. Truly she was a living witness to the fact that it was here in these parts that the Roman legions first planted the Eagle banner and set up their camp.

'What tidings have you brought us?' asked the Abbess, when the peasant girl had knelt before her and kissed the hem of her gown.

'My name is Bajka Petrino', she answered softly, with dignified composure, 'and I am a widow. Like all the rest, I too was for Mikulev and would have given him any help I could against the soldiery, but now, since he shows no respect for Holy Church, since he does not shrink from stealing God's sacred vessels, like a good Christian woman I renounce him and all his ways, and I am willing to hand him over to the law.'

'How so? Do you know him well then?' asked the Abbess.

'No. I have never seen him, or exchanged a single word with him. But for all that, I can catch him for you whenever I like.'

'I believe you could', said Voinescu with a smile.

'And what do you ask from us in return?' enquired the Abbess.

'As far as I am concerned,—I could do with a new sheep-skin.'

'And what form of assistance do you want us to give you?'

'I need no help of any kind. I will deliver him into your hands. Just leave it to me.'

Chance came to the aid of the beautiful widow. A rich farmer, Jeremy Galescu, in accordance with ancient custom, sent two matchmakers to her and sued for her hand in marriage. She was not content to decline the brandy they brought with them, whereby the matter would officially have been at an end anyway, but even added insult to injury by telling them : 'I would have accepted Galescu, willingly, for I have nothing against him, but as it happens my taste runs higher. There's only one man in the land to whom I would give myself—Mikulev. If ever I am to serve another husband, he will have to be a hero.'

When Bajka spoke these words, she was perfectly well aware that they would reach the ears of Mikulev, and actually, not long after this, an old woman, with piercing eyes and dishevelled hair under her red head-scarf,—none other than the village witch, in fact—came to her and whispered that the notorious robber would visit her that night.

As the watchman trumpeted the midnight call, there was a tap at Bajka's window. She opened it and a slender, handsome fellow in the picturesque Carpathian garb, with dagger and pistols in his belt and a musket in his hand, sprang into the room. The young widow looked at him in astonishment. She liked him only too well, and for a moment she was almost sorry she was pledged to deliver him to the gallows,—but only for a moment.

'You expressed a desire for me?' said the robber, while his admiring glance looked the young woman's superb figure up and down. 'Well, here I am.'

'Are you Mikulev?'

'Do you imagine anyone else would have had the courage to come to you, at this time, when they are lying in wait for me and my men on all sides?'

He stood his musket in the corner, sat himself down on the chimney-seat and pulled Bajka on to his lap. 'You are pretty', he murmured, 'and you know it. However, I am sure I am not the first to have told you that.'

'But I'd rather hear it from you than from anyone else.'

While she submitted quietly to his caresses, nothing could be heard in the little room but the busy gnawing of a mouse. When the robber had satiated himself with the beautiful widow's kisses, he drew from his breast two strings of magnificent coral beads and presented them to her with a proud smile.

She was as pleased as a child with this ornament, and when he then made her a present of a pair of costly ear-

" 'You have no need of finery to steal a man's heart and soul.' " (p. 54)

rings she blushed with pride, sprang up and cavorted before the mirror that hung on the wall and began preening herself, while he was taking off and laying aside his weapons.

'How do I look to you now?' she asked, as she came and stood in front of him.

'You have no need of finery to steal a man's heart and soul.'

'Are you in love with me then?' she said artfully and threw her soft, seductive arms around his neck. He simply looked at her and nodded.

A table was laid and now they sat down at it.

Mikulev recounted to her some of his deeds and adventures and the young widow listened enthralled.

'But why did you rob Holy Church?' she interjected. 'How can you justify that before God and Man?'

'Before God?—Do you think he looks upon the vessels in which the Eucharist is offered? What does he care for gold and silver? He sees men's deeds, he looks into their hearts and judges them accordingly. He is not deceived by prayer and incense. What are these priests, these monks and nuns, except a bunch of liars and hypocrites? To us they promise the Kingdom of Heaven, but they are clever enough to keep the earth for themselves, and while we go hungry and homeless and cold, they wax fat at our expense and commit all those sins for which they keep Hell hot for us.'

Once again Bajka felt overcome with remorse for a moment. She wavered and was on the point of rescinding her resolution.

'Now, my pretty one', began the robber anew, 'listen to me. I have no time to lose. I cannot send matchmakers to you, exchange rings with you, or have our union blessed by the Pope. You are my wife before God, so what more can we want? You are mine and shall stay mine.'

'As soon as I say "yes"', answered Bajka provokingly. Her pride rebelled against the idea of giving any man her love who had not first wooed her,—who, as it were, crudely took her by storm, as a paser-by might pluck a wild rose.

'Shall I perhaps come and lie outside your window at night?' asked the robber, laughing. 'Shall I serenade you? Dance the *hora** with you? Or maybe you would like me to serve you for seven years, like Jacob and his lovely Rachel?'

'I don't ask for such things', said she patiently, 'but if you are proud, so am I. I *give* my love, I let no man steal it from me.'

Mikulev leapt to his feet and laughingly picked her up in his strong arms.

'Now, are you going to fight for your honour—are you?'

She saw that she was in his power, and so she shrugged it off with a laugh, for she knew that the next moment he would be in hers, just as soon as she wished,—and she wished it now, for all at once she had made up her mind.

'Now, will you be mine?' demanded the robber.

'Yes, I will,' was her answer. And as he put her down on her feet again, she calmly smoothed her rumpled hair and her embroidered chemise, and stroked with both hands the black lamb's-wool of her short jacket.

'Come', she told him; picked up the small dim light that resembled a hanging lamp from a Roman tomb, and went ahead of him to the bedroom. He followed her, pretending to be in no hurry, and stepped—as she had foreseen he would, having laid her plan carefully before-hand—on to the trap-door and plunged with a muffled shout into a kind of wolf-pit below.

'So,—now I've got you! Do you still think to take me by force? You are my slave now, and I can do what I like with you.'

'Would you destroy me?' called the robber from the depths.

'I have sworn to rid the country of you', she answered, 'and I intend to keep my word.'

'You mean you are going to deliver me to the enemies of the people?'

'Yes, and I will see you hanged.'

**Hora:* Rumanian country dance.

She turned back into the living-room, picked up one of his pistols and fired through the open window. It was not long before the gendarmes marched in and put the robber in chains.

As Mikulev was led up to the gallows, Bajka stood erect in her little ox-drawn cart and nodded to him. She was wearing the new sheepskin that the Abbess had given her, the coral-bead necklace and ear-rings that the robber had presented her with. At her feet stood two bags of gold, the price that the government had placed on the robber's head.

GIRLS WHO WHIP MEN

. . . Yet there was nothing fierce or satanic about this little Seraphita who, with titillating words and the enigmatic reticences of the initiated, was telling us about these strange happenings, during one of those after-dinner sessions that go on and on through the haze of cigar-smoke.

Her tomboyish face framed with ringlets of golden silk like a halo of light, her roguish little nose, her velvety cheeks tinged with sudden flushes, her lips parting every now and then in joyous or in mischievous smiles, she seemed scarcely a woman at all, but a little girl rather well developed for her age and whose ingenuous heart has been spared the buffeting that comes from contact with life and whose most cherished illusions have not been stripped of their blossom by the rough wind of circumstance.

Only her eyes, gleaming with the changing glint of some precious stone—from the dark blue that derives from profoundest depths to the merciless azure of summer skies—the pupils of which, by turns, lit up, turned metallic, or became impregnated with hints of cruelties, dark imaginings, or some vague, depraved recollection, suggested a certain disorder, a certain abnormal complication, in the working of the simple, charming soul of that schoolgirlish creature whose virginal flesh still slumbered unsullied.

We had smiled at first—as at an amusing interlude—while she elaborated her theories about Love, punctuated with bursts of violent mimicry, to which she added the savour of the guttural, drawling accent, rough yet at the same time coaxing, of a natural nomad born under canvas; then she would become fidgety and break off suddenly, frowning and grinding her teeth in a mouth set in a petulant pout.

And there we sat, each of us leaning his elbows on the table, on which there stood a confusion of sticky glasses and bottles, listening with a sort of instinctive uneasiness, fascinated by those unknown depravities of which she had made herself the apostle, the mirages of Eden, the Promised Land, in her staring eyes, seductiveness in her long, white, supple hands, the imperious hands of a priestess . . .

'So', Seraphita was saying, her pale cheeks tinted with red by the pounding of her heart, 'you think you are lovers and that you give proof of your love for a woman just because, for weeks, for months, for years even, you cleave to her more closely than to any other; you flatter her, you implore her in sentimental, fervent expressions, hoping that your words may weave a magic spell, that intoxicating perfumes and sweet melodies may unite in harmony with the desire that goads you on unrelentingly, with the passion that gnaws you to the marrow of your bones,—like that deceptive tunic soaked in the blood of monsters in which the god Hercules fought his battles; just because your mouth is rivited to hers; because you carry her away into torpid ecstasies; because you obey her, you succumb to a sort of bondage, you abdicate your will-power, you kneel under the yoke her proffering fingers hold out to you, you pay, now with sufferings, now with nostalgic regrets, now with tears, for whatever the Excessively Loved One grants you by way of beatitudes and bliss!

'But what, after all, is this game of slow corruption in which it seems the heart is merely debased, polluted, stifled in bestial practices, or in which, to reach the desired goal, one takes the same road as the generality of men, as those who are nothing but blind forces without a single spark of intelligence in their brain, which only so very slightly differentiates them from animals trained to work for man,—the road that leads at last, through debauchery, to annihilation. What are these ephemeral sensual delights, these ludicrous comedies, compared with what our anxious, insatiable, searching Slavonic souls have discovered—compared with the enjoyments offered by the élite to whom woman—the virgin—is the sovereign idol!—compared with those real torments to which the devotees condemn themselves, abandon themselves, in proof of their complete submission and in order to testify to their fervour!'

In her pale blue pupils flashed a radiant succession of memories; then, more slowly, as if to make her words, one by one, sink into our brain and remain embedded for ever, she went on:

'I expect you have all read at some time or other on the fourth page of the big Hungarian and Russian newspapers enigmatic announcements worded something like this: 'PRETTY GIRL, beats all comers ... ' followed by some address or other. This simply means that Miss X or Miss Y is a member of our cult and, if she finds the man who writes to her imploringly and comes to the agreed rendezvous interesting and pleasing, is ready and willing to become the mistress who will dominate him, grant him the delights of physical suffering, the dreams of Paradise that will make him like one of those saints of old whose flesh was purified by being incessantly mortified; she will soundly flagellate him with the frenzy of an executioner pitilessly flogging his victim.

'Then, if this form of "marriage" is contracted, they get together in some apartment which is thickly carpeted and hung with heavy material covering the walls so as to deaden the cries and groans. The man partly undresses, lays himself down, his torso bare, on some wild animal skin, offers the girl his wrists and ankles to fetter with rings and chains, allowing her to reduce him to utter impotence. And she, her breasts exposed, her low-cut white evening gown thrown back, her fingers gripping the handle of a riding-whip, exerts all her strength upon the being who is now in her power, strikes him with all her might, strikes again and again, and goes on striking, infatuated with her task, intoxicated by those cries of love distraught, by those sobs of adoration, by those hoarse moans of suffering that ascend towards her towering beauty, by the blood that flows, that fills the room, as it were, with the odour of a burnt offering. In a kind of holy frenzy she glares with flashing eyes into those of her victim, who gazes at her devouringly, caressing her, so to speak, through a mist of tears; she stares at that flesh, aware that he is at her mercy: his entire soul, his very thoughts, belong to her.

'She wishes that her weak feminine frame, her arms, her muscles, had more formidable vigour, that her strength could last for ever, could be multiplied tenfold, so that she could flog and flog until he died from it, expired beside her, his heart broken, his pupils extinguished.'

'To hell with that! What an idea, mademoiselle!' stammered Laumières, speaking thickly like one who has awakened with a start in the middle of a nightmare. 'You may go on like that all you want, but that sort of thing doesn't tempt *me*—not in the least!'

La Glandée, who was agitatedly wiping the steamed-up glass of his monocle, sat up straight and, anxious as ever to learn something new, to get, as he put it, to the bottom of things, asked:

'Are there very many of you in your little flagellating confraternity?'

Seraphita appeared not to notice the point of irony that barbed this question, and replied feverishly:

'Since we never meet except in couples, I can't see how that can matter anyway. And was it not one of your greatest poets who said that what made Paradise such a happy place was the small number of the Elect? . . . A hundred, or a thousand, or more . . . but, and this is the strangest part about it, among the most determined, the keenest adherents one finds, in particular, robust, healthy young fellows, built like powerful wrestlers ready for the fray, those handsome, blond, pink-cheeked officers with square shoulders and chests bulging like bucklers,— yes, heaps of officers, who could knock us down with the merest flick of their fingers and yet who, looking forward to this mystic martyrdom, can no longer bring themselves to want any other kind of love and are avidly on the look-out for those suggestive advertisements I spoke of just now!'

Then the girl added sadly:

'But alas! not one of you gentlemen finds me beautiful and loves me, for neither you, M. de Laumières, nor you, M. La Glandée, flirtatious though you are, nor George Vignolles, asks to be put to the test or offers himself to my whip!'

'That, Mademoiselle Seraphita, my delightful little angel', La Glandée suggested, 'is where your little festivities are too lacking in ... how shall I put it? ... They have no continuation, no ending. We are not yet sufficiently far gone, you see; and, as far as I'm concerned, to be perfectly truthful I prefer my own little darling—yes, indeed, by Jove! I'd rather have her any day!'

Seraphita shrugged her shoulders.

VARVARA PAGADIN

A TALE OF THE RUSSIAN WAY OF LIFE

Just as great thoughts mature best in the propitious peace and quiet of solitude, so a truly tremendous passion may well develop more uninhibitedly in the midst of simple circumstances than in the rushing stream of urban life. Thus it was that in a small Ukrainian village set well away from the great highways, Varvara Pagadin came to know the student Semen Pultovsky and their hearts became united for ever. Varvara was the daughter of a tenant farmer. Through the influence of a girl friend of hers, who was studying medicine in Kiev and from time to time came home on visits to her parents, Varvara became inoculated with the love of freedom, and correspondingly a hatred of tyranny and Tsarism, and with these the urge to take her place, through hard work and education, as an equal at the side of men. So Varvara studied and read untiringly, and forthwith began to turn the results of her efforts to good account. She professed herself a nihilist and joined the great and intrepid political party, which, in Russia, seeks to destroy all existing organisations, and until this achieved, contents itself with uplifting the common sense of people, broadening their general knowledge, and rooting out the prejudices and superstitions that make of them a herd of slaves obedient to the despotism of State and Church.

For all this, she was indeed too much a woman not to set about re-fashioning the world in her own extrovert manner; but it was certainly not womanly vanity that guided the hands of this lovely girl to cut off her own luxuriant fair hair, which when it was untied flowed around her like a mantle of gold,—but, from now on, so close-cropped it was and such an air of stern asceticism did it impart to her, that she looked much more like a young theologian than a captivating love-goddess. She invariably walked about now in her high boots, a frock devoid of any ornament, a plain jacket, and with a round masculine hat on her head—in fact, the living picture of a modern Amazon who despises the trappings of feminine coquettishness. She had acquired sufficient medical knowledge from her studies to be quite capable of playing the role of a doctor and a Sister of Mercy, not just in the village itself but in the whole region for miles around, where no general practitioner was to be found; but this did not satisfy her. In her father's house she set up a village school in which she gave instruction, not only to the local children but to the grown-ups as well; she taught them reading, writing and arithmetic, and in addition imparted to them the most essential notions concerning the universe, the laws of nature, the earth and its inhabitants, and the destiny of mankind. Besides all this, she wrote articles for periodicals and gave the farmers useful information concerning the cultivation of the land and livestock. On horseback, seated astride in the saddle like a man, she ranged the countryside and was soon spoken of in every district.

It was in the midst of this feverish activity that she met Semen Pultovsky, who was studying chemistry at Kiev; at the time of their meeting he was spending the Easter holiday in the home of his father, a tax-collector. They began by practising together firing pistols at a target and fencing with rapiers, and finished up by falling deeply in love with each other. Such was the ascetic nature of their striving and their goal, that in both their hearts there was a glowing aspiration towards the good and noble, but in addition they were children of nature with something of the wildness of the Little Russian stock about them. Their love, therefore, was no purposeful choice for pleasure's sake, no rationalised self-seeking, assuredly no blissfully sentimental roving by moonlight, and least of all a frivolous game: it was ruggedly elemental in character.

Semen went back to Kiev, to resume his studies; but

when the holiday months came and he was with his parents once more, the bond between him and this intrepid, energetic girl became day by day stronger and deeper. Semen Pultovsky, too, belonged to the Russian subversive party, had become an active participant at various levels, and had taken part on numerous occasions in more or less hazardous enterprises.

While on his way back to Kiev in the autumn to renew his studies, he took part in a mass demonstration, and, with a number of other students, was arrested.

Varvara Pagadin learned of this through the newspaper; she read the shocking news twice, without betraying the slightest agitation: as she folded the newspaper and laid it aside, however, her resolution was already made. She packed a small suitcase, climbed into her father's *britschka*, to which two small lean horses were harnessed, drove to the nearest railway station and, the next morning, she was in Kiev.

Just what she was after or expected to do, she herself could not explain, but somehow she felt her presence there was necessary. Some mysterious, fatalistic urge was driving her onward.

She rented a room in the house of an officer's widow, and unpacked. The first thing she did after that was look for work. She found very quickly, within the first few days, a job in a small but elegant shop that sold gloves and cravats. If Varvara had been even slightly experienced in the ways of the world, not just a few circumstances but indeed everything about this business would have aroused her suspicions: the room behind the shop furnished with every refinement and luxury; the proprietress of the establishment, Marfa Ivanovna, clad in stiff, rustling silks and perfumed with musk; the pretty, heavily made-up girls ornate in low-necked dresses; the elegant gentlemen who flirtatiously exchanged enigmatic glances with them,—but Varvara was only a simple country girl and gathered nothing sinister from all this; she gave the men brief, polite answers to their enquiries and served them with handkerchiefs, ties and scarves, without misgivings.

At night, she would prowl about outside the police building in the hope of catching a glimpse of her beloved behind one of the barred windows.

One evening, when there was no one in the shop but Marfa Ivanovna and herself, the former having, under some pretext or other, got Varvara to stay behind, a tall, handsome man suddenly entered, wrapped in an expensive fur coat, and his fascinating grey eyes fastened at once upon Varvara.

'What can we do for you at this late hour, Seraf Pavlovich?' said Marfa Ivanovna, curtseying with exaggerated humility.

'A pair of gloves', replied the late arrival slowly. Varvara placed the box on the counter in front of him and Marfa Ivanovna exchanged a few words with him in a low voice.

'You're from the country, Miss?' began the stranger.

'That is so.'

'And how do you like it here in the city?'

'I have found work here; I am content.'

'Ah, you shall find something more than that', pursued the man. 'But who has been guilty of such an act of vandalism as to cut off that lovely hair?'

'I did it myself.'

'One might almost take you for a nihilist', he went on, smiling. 'But women of that sort are all ugly.'

Varvara turned red. The stranger had meanwhile chosen a pair of gloves. He spoke:

'I am pleased to have made your acquaintance, Miss— er, what is your name?'

'Varvara Pagadin.'

'Miss Varvara. I hope we shall meet again.'

He took his leave of her, and even raised his hat a little. Marfa Ivanovna accompanied him to the door, where he said something to her in a subdued voice.

'What luck!' exclaimed Marfa Ivanovna, when she had shut the door behind him. 'He likes you, you have quite captivated him,—him of all people—before whom we all tremble.'

'And who might he be?'

'Why, Seraf Pavlovich Halikov, of course,—who else? The man who was in here just now. The Chief of Police in Kiev.'

'Why didn't you say so before?' exclaimed Varvara, and all at once her mind was made up.

'Now, now we mustn't be in too much of a hurry.'

'And he likes me, you say?'

'He has fallen madly in love with you, my little dove, that I can tell you. But you will have to dress differently and do your hair a different way: above all, you must buy yourself some plaits. At the moment you look as if you had just come out of jail. Do you need any money?'

'No, thanks, but—'

'What is it, sweetheart? You can trust me . . .'

'Oh, well, just tell him,—the Chief of Police, I mean,— that I like him too. D'you know what I'm trying to say . . . I like him tremendously.'

'I'll let him know, you may be sure.'

The very next evening, Halikov saw Varvara home. She still wore her simple clothes, but now she had put some false hair on her head and looked more lovely than ever. The Chief of Police took one look at her dingy little room and her one paltry suitcase and summed up the situation immediately.

'A girl from the country', he began, 'is, in town, exposed to manifold temptations: please allow me in some small measure to play the part of Providence and look after you. First of all, you shall not go to Marfa Ivanovna's any more. She is a person of bad reputation.'

'In what respect?'

'She conducts a shameful traffic in beauty and innocence.'

Varvara Pagadin stared at him incredulously, unable to grasp his meaning.

'What is more, you can't stay here in this room any

longer', Halikov went on,—'providing you don't find my interest in your welfare objectionable . . . '

'I have made up my mind to do whatever you advise.'

'So much the better. There's no need, then, to waste another word over life's trivialities; just you leave everything to me.'

'I agree willingly to that, in fact I shall be most grateful.'

'It is I who should be grateful to you, Varvara.'

During the afternoon of the following day, Halikov came with a carriage and conducted Varvara to the new apartment that he had taken for her and charmingly appointed in genuine Parisian style. She found there an elderly chambermaid, a chef, and a liveried footman, at her command, while in the small drawing-room Madame Puthon, the proprietress of one of the most distinguished fashion-houses, and Alex Tilmonich, Kiev's leading jeweller, were waiting to serve her. Both laid out their precious wares before her, and as Varvara was evidently somewhat out of her depth, Halikov, with the assistance of Madame Puthon, chose for her an exciting négligé, as well as a number of outfits for the open air, and placed several other orders on the spot, while he also bought for her from the jeweller a pair of expensive ear-rings, two bracelets and a costly gold crucifix.

Later the same evening, Varvara Pagadin received a mysterious note. It said: 'You are as shrewd as you are courageous. We have every confidence in you. You have embarked upon the right way, not only to free Semen Pultovsky, but also to provide the very greatest assistance to our cause. Await further instructions from us before you act. You will be given every assistance that lies within our power.'

Varvara tossed the letter into the fire. A few moments later the Chief of Police came in.

A week had gone by; a second came and went, and then another message arrived.

'Do not count on rescuing Semen Pultovsky; you can avenge him but you cannot secure his freedom.'

And two days later, Varvara Pagadin received a "death warrant"—for Seraf Pavlovich Halikov, Kiev's Chief of Police—together with the command to execute sentence of death within three days. She hid the terrible document in her bodice, stepped up to the mirror, tidied her hair, and then rang for her maid to dress her.

When Halikov came to the apartment to dine with her, he found her reclining on her ottoman in a half-lying, half-sitting position, wearing a white silk dressing-gown, trimmed with white fox fur, in the style of Sarah Bernhardt.

'You look marvellous!' he began, when he had kissed her hand,— 'but why are your hands so cold?'

'I am afraid.'

'Of what?'

'I don't know, really. But I feel I must have a dagger.'

'A dagger? Wouldn't this be better for you?' and Halikov produced a small revolver from his pocket and handed it to her.

'It will do for the time being,—but you will bring me a dagger, won't you?'

'If you say so.'

After dinner, Halikov went to sleep as usual on a couch in the dining-room. Varvara sat in a small armchair by the fireside. She regarded him fixedly for some time, then suddenly got up, stepped lightly across the deep-pile carpet, stood before him, raised the revolver, held it against his temple, and then lowered it again. 'I can't kill him in his sleep', she said to herself; 'that would be too cowardly.'

That same night he brought her the dagger, and she stuck it in her belt. As they were drinking tea, she drew the weapon, unobserved by him, resolved to strike the mortal blow, but again she did not do so.

'I must take courage', she told herself the next morning, when she woke up amid the soft pillows, 'for it is today that the great deed must be done.'

She waited in vain, however, for the Police Chief to come to lunch with her: he did not appear until late afternoon, but when he did he was in buoyant humour.

'You're in very high spirits', she said; 'what's happened, Seraf Pavlovich?'

'I have had a really choice catch today', he retorted, with a cold smile; 'we raided a printing-works belonging to the nihilists.'

Chance had come to Varvara's aid.

'You must have many prisoners already', she said calmly. 'Aren't you short of space by now?'

'We just pack 'em in like sardines', replied Halikov. 'There's never any question of inconvenience.'

'What has happened to Semen Pultovsky?'

'You know him?'

'He is from the same village as I.'

'He's still alive, although I have repeatedly interrogated him with the utmost severity. It's that sort of stubborn young fellow who refuses to confess that I like best.'

'How so? I'm afraid I don't follow.'

'Because I can have them flogged to my heart's content.'

Varvara turned pale and a slight shudder convulsed her.

'Don't you feel any pity for these poor souls?'

'Pity? No!' answered Halikov with deliberation, and as though he were weighing every word; 'I experience much more pleasure, a pleasure like that which I feel when you are lying in my arms, Varvara.'

'Do you hate these nihilists so much?'

'It's not that; there are others I would just as soon have in my power.' His grey eyes glowed coldly like a tiger's. 'It's a source of great enjoyment to me to see them trembling before me and to watch how fear makes the blood flush their pale cheeks. D'you understand that, Varvara?'

'Oh yes, I do!' she exclaimed, her eyes flashing; 'I am sure I could find pleasure in that too. Take me with you, Seraf Pavlovich, let me be a witness at such a scene.'

'Why not?' said he. 'I'll arrange things in such a way that you will be able to see everything without being seen yourself.'

'You promise?'

'I give you my word.'

'And can I go with you this very day?'

'No; tomorrow, Varvara,—and to make it more interesting for you, and more to your taste, I dare say, I'll arrange for this fellow whom you know—this Pultovsky—to be interrogated.'

The third day had come. By midnight the death sentence must be carried out, or Varvara would be lost: she knew that. With the advent of darkness, Halikov came in a carriage to fetch her. She wrapped herself in a magnificent sable coat, covered her head with a gold-embroidered *bashlik** and clapped her dagger to her side. On the way, Halikov was turning over in his mind the question as to which would give him more pleasure—to torture his unfortunate victim himself, or to be a witness to the impression the young man's sufferings made on his beautiful mistress, who, despite the thick furs in which she was warmly enveloped, was trembling at his side as though with cold.

He decided on the former course. After showing Varvara into a dark closet, from which she was able to step unseen into a great wall-cupboard (like a wardrobe) and observe perfectly, through two small openings, all that went on in the adjoining interrogation room, Halikov betook himself into the latter, in which it was as cold as in the depths of Siberia, made himself comfortable, in his thick fur coat, at the table on which stood a crucifix between two candles; then he ordered Semen Pultovsky to be brought in.

Varvara turned deadly white, and tears filled her eyes, as her beloved, ashen pale, emaciated, broken, in thin clothing and shivering with cold, staggered in, laden with chains.

'How are you, Semen Pultovsky?'

The unfortunate rebel shrugged his shoulders.

'Have you changed your mind yet? Have you thought better of it? Are you ready to confess now?'

* *Bashlik:* a hood or head-covering as worn in Russia and some other countries.

'I have nothing to confess.'

'Don't infuriate me!'

'I have no wish to do so', replied Pultovsky with a sigh, 'but I know nothing, and so . . . '

'Dog! Talk . . . here and now! D'you hear me?' Halikov sprang up, and dragging Pultovsky by the hair threw him to the floor and kicked him. 'Now, confess! Confess at once!'

'I cannot—I am innocent!' groaned the poor wretch.

'Innocent!' sniggered Halikov. 'Give him the knout!'

The constables bound him to the iron ring that was fixed to the wall, and one of them began to flog him.

There was an expression of devilish delight on Halikov's handsome face as he watched the punishment.

It was late that evening when the Chief of Police returned with Varvara to her apartment. A carriage stood outside the house and two strangers were pacing up and down the pavement.

When they reached her quarters, Varvara told Halikov to wait a moment, went into her bedroom, threw off her heavy fur and quickly slipped on a comfortable red jacket trimmed with marten fur, which did not hinder her movements in the least; then she called the Police Chief to her.

As he entered, she stood in the centre of the room, her arms folded across her breast.

'Do you know who the man is whom you have just had flogged?' she began coldly.

'Semen Pultovsky.'

'He was my lover.'

'Ah! If only I had known!'

'What then?'

'Then I would have got still more pleasure out of it.'

'Do not insult me, Seraf Pavlovich! You shall never ill-treat another living soul!'

'Oh, no? And why not?'

'Read this.'

She handed him the death warrant, and scarcely had he

71

"She handed him the death warrant and ... buried her
dagger in his chest."

had time to peruse it when she buried her dagger in his chest. He collapsed at her feet without a sound, but the next moment he tried to get up and to call for help. No cry came from his lips, however, but only a trickle of blood.

Varvara raised the dagger again.

'Mercy!' muttered Halikov.

'Have you shown mercy to me? Did you have any mercy for Semen Pultovsky?' she replied, with an icy sneer. A second thrust with the dagger brought his life to an end.

As Varvara calmly wiped the weapon on her victim's clothing, an elegantly-dressed man, his hat on his head, a pistol in his hand, entered the room.

'Is the task completed?' he enquired.

'Yes.'

'Is he dead?'

'There he is—see for yourself.'

'Come along then, quickly. Quickly!'

He offered Varvara his arm, and while other men, armed with daggers and revolvers, guarded the doors and the staircase, he hurried out with Varvara, ushered her into the waiting carriage and slammed the door. The coachman whipped up the horses.

A few moments later, there was a great commotion upstairs; police thronged into the house and found Halikov murdered.

Pultovsky died in prison. Varvara is still wanted by the Russian police. She has, quite simply, disappeared.

THE RED MANOR-HOUSE

On a gentle rise in the centre of the village of Bialagora
there stands a pretty country mansion, which in those
parts is known to everyone as 'The Red Manor-House'.
It is a quiet, peaceful corner,—a more peaceful one,
indeed, could scarcely be imagined. The masonry is every-
where as gleaming white as if it were covered with fresh-
fallen snow and the roof glows blood-red amid the sur-
rounding greenness, for everything round about is green,
—the creepers and the vine branches that cover the buildings, the trellises and arbours, the ancient lime-trees,
the fruit-trees that surround the lordly manor, the very
village, which is like one huge garden, the stunted
meadows standing on the banks of the stream, and the
round hillock itself on which the cattle graze. And while
everything on all sides look fresh and green, at all times
too one hears merry, friendly voices: the lark sings joy-
fully, the quail calls, the swallows twitter clinging to their
nests, or the stork clatters behind the farmhouse chimney;
and even when all else is silent the crickets still chirp in
the ancient walls.

Peaceful and amicable, too, are the lord of the manor,
Pan Kochansky, and the peasants of Bialagora, who live
together as good neighbours.

No one any longer has any inkling of what frightful
scenes have been enacted here, and when anyone talks
of them, people shake their heads and will scarcely believe
that it is by no means from its red roof that this manor-
house takes its name.

It was not yet that most distressing of all times in
Galicia, though the then nobility of Polish stock assuredly
imposed a harsh régime, keeping their vassals down with

74

a rod of iron, but at the same time allowing them to live fairly well within their straitened circumstances. The real aggressors of the peasantry were those masters of a later period who, while they slunk on tiptoe into milady's drawing-room down-at-heel and with holes in their threadbare hose, they strutted about the village liberally dispensing kicks with their bespurred and muddy riding-boots; and those ladies whose tiny hands, framed in costly furs, might be flicking over the pages of Byron's *Manfred* at one moment and the next instant lash out with some vicious instrument of castigation.

The old lord, Bogratski, lived with his wife, their servants, (who in those days were often born and died in the same house), their peasants, horses, cattle, geese and pigs, in as patriarchal a fashion as any Abraham or Ulysses. When, however, the younger Bogratski, Vladislav, on the death of his father, took the reins of power into his hands, things straightway became very different, very different indeed. Yet not exactly at once, as it happened.

At first he brought a young wife home who was a real angel, both as regards outward appearance and in her whole being, and so long as she was there things were not in the least any worse than before. But one day the angel unfurled her wings and flew away—with none other than a handsome young Frenchman who had introduced himself on his arrival in Bialagora as a viscount, but, as it turned out later, was in reality only a Parisian barber.

So much did he despise her that from then on Vladislav Bogratski nursed a bitter hatred of mankind (though, despite his best intentions, he couldn't quite manage to hate women).

Byron was his favourite poet, but secretly he devoured Pushkin and Lermontov also, though he, as a Pole, in those days of mutual bitterness dare not openly admire anything Russian.

Nurtured in part by his distrust of everyone and in part by the effects of the almost despotic power which he had wielded over his subjects for nearly thirty years, a Neronian streak became more and more evident in his character,—a cruel pleasure derived from the sufferings of others, and the desire to do them violence, to ill-treat and persecute.

He was soon held in awe throughout the region as the most dangerous type of Don Juan: he was no subtle seducer who intoxicated women by his personal charm, or who, by the whispering of sweet nothings, or the fascination of his eloquence, beguiled them into some devilish passion; he was a crude tyrant who took possession of any woman by sheer brute force, and, when he had satiated himself with her, cast her aside entirely without pity or compunction.

He had already left behind him a long trail of erotic interludes with peasant girls and Jewesses, noblewomen and actresses, when one day, in late autumn, as he was returning from a hunt, he suddenly saw standing at the door of a small, humble cottage in his village a young peasant lass of extraordinary beauty. As the girl greeted him with the traditional salutation: 'Blessed be Jesus Christ', Bogratski found himself spontaneously murmuring the lines of Lermontov's gloomy poem:

> Life's gilded cup is filled with wine,
> We quaff it down unthinking;
> The tippler heeds no teardrops' brine
> Clouding the draught he's drinking,
> Till he falls victim, eyes unbound,
> To Death's relentless capture.
> Then vanish all the things he found
> That ever gave him rapture;
> The drinker then can clearly see
> The wine was an illusion,
> And knows how helplessly was he
> Besotted by delusion.

He acknowledged the girl's greeting with a haughty, sardonic smile; the next moment he gazed full into the finely-chiselled features of her face with its mischievous dark eyes, and found himself utterly bewitched.

'What's your name?' he asked.

'Maruvka Kostecki.'

As she, like any other peasant woman, did not let her hair hang down in long plaits in the cold weather but had a red scarf bound round her head and was wearing an old sheepskin round her shoulders, he could not be sure whether it was a married woman who stood before him, or not.

'Where's your husband?' he went on.

'I'm not married', she replied.

'Oh. And have you a lover?'

Maruvka blushed blood-red and cast her eyes to the ground.

'Who *is* your lover?'

'Sergei Kostalko.'

'And are you betrothed to him?' he continued relentlessly.

'Yes.'

'With all your heart?'

'With all my heart.'

'I'm glad of that', pursued Bogratski with a diabolical smile. 'You shall come to my house this evening. Do you understand? We must wait and see what will happen after that.'

'God will reward you, sir', said Maruvka and kissed his hand. He let her do so, and at the same time touched her forehead with his lips.

'When shall I come, sir?'

'As soon as it's dark.' He waved to her and rode on.

When Maruvka, as the first star appeared, was making her way towards the manor-house, she met Sergei.

'Where are you going?' he asked.

'To the manor-house.'

'Who to?'

'To the lord of the manor.'

'Are you out of your mind? D'you realise what you're letting yourself in for?'

'The lord means well with us.'

'I'll tell you what'll happen,' Sergi went on. 'The lord

will keep you in his house, dressed in fine clothes, for his own pleasure; and when he doesn't fancy you any more, he'll want to marry us,—only I won't do it, I tell you. You can bear your shame alone.'

'Don't worry', said the girl. 'I'd rather die than be unfaithful to you.'

As the *valet de chambre* led her into the great lord's room, there he lay like some oriental Pasha reclining on a Turkish divan; he took his long pipe out of his mouth and contemplated her with an expression of ironic satisfaction. Then with a wave of his slim, well-manicured hand he dismissed the lackey . . .

When Maruvka left the room, she was consumed with fire. She looked shyly and enviously around her, and hastily bound up into a plait her hair which was all undone.

She never left the manor-house. She was kept there like a prisoner,—but like an imprisoned princess or a favourite concubine in a harem.

Day and night poor Sergei slunk about around the house but could not manage to speak to her. More than three weeks had gone by when he caught his first glimpse of her and even then only from a distance. Bogratski was just dismounting from his horse, and Maruvka was standing at the door watching him. She was still dressed in country style, but in costly and beautiful material that gave her the appearance of the wife of some Turkish official of a bygone century. The red boots on her feet blended perfectly with her short frock of a gaily-coloured Turkish fabric and her blue bodice from which frothed the dazzling white lace of her shift. Over all this she was wearing a long open coat of pale blue satin adorned and padded with grey Siberian squirrel.

From her neck hung necklaces of coral and gold coins reaching down to her well-rounded breasts, while a band of red silk, like a turban, was bound round her black hair.

Bogratski leaned down from the saddle to kiss her, then

sprang to the ground and Maruvka greeted him with a warm smile. Sergei crept along behind the rose-bushes that surrounded the house, but at the very moment that he drew level with her, she, quite unaware of his presence, went back into the house, and the Cossack groom, who was polishing harness in the yard, drove him off with sharp words and curses.

Another time, when snow had already fallen, she found Sergei in the courtyard. Maruvka tried to evade him, but he held her in his grasp.

'What are you afraid of?' he began. 'Have you a guilty conscience?'

'Let me go!'

'Not before you tell me yourself whether you belong to the lord of the manor or to me.'

'What can a poor girl do against his power?'

'All right then: flee with me into the mountains!' he shouted.

'I wouldn't dream of it,' was her amused reply. 'I'm doing very well here.'

'Maruvka, have you no fear of the wrath of God?' said Sergei, with tears in his eyes.

'You poor fool!' she cried, glancing scornfully at him. 'Who says there *is* a God? The lord says that God exists only for peasants, not for us.'

'Are you out of your mind?'

'*You* are. Now leave me alone.' She started to call for help.

He drew his knife, and tried to stab her, but his thrust missed; then Bogratski, who happened to come by at that moment, seized his arm and his men overpowered Sergei and tied his hands behind his back.

'You know what will happen to you now, don't you?' began Maruvka, with a malicious grin. 'You will be hanged.'

'No, my dear', interrupted Bogratski. 'He shall not get off so lightly.'

He gave orders for the whipping-bench to be set up in the courtyard and for Sergei to be strapped on it. As his two Cossack servants began their cruel task of beating him with rods, he and Maruvka stood in the doorway of the house and watched. She looked a little pale, but a satisfied smile hovered upon her lips.

When Sergei had received a hundred strokes, he lay still, like one devoid of life. Nobody in the mansion paid any further attention to him.

A sympathetic old woman took him to his hut. She was said to be a witch, and, as far as he was concerned, she did indeed perform a miracle. She not only saved his life, but within a short time even restored him completely to health and strength. Hardly did Bogratski hear, however, that the poor fellow was well again when he ordered him to come to the manor-house once more.

It was night-time when he was brought in. In the great hall where Bogratski entertained his guests sat Maruvka upon a low divan, bathing her feet. Now she was dressed and her hair curled like a real lady and, deceptively beautiful, she looked just like a genuine Polish aristocrat in her sumptuous green velvet *kazabaika* trimmed with marten fur. No less dazzling was Bogratski's appearance. He was a tall, slender man with perfect symmetry of limbs and a countenance like an Adonis; the nightgown he was wearing, of pale blue silk adorned with ermine, set off to perfection the fresh, delicate colour of the fur and the rich blond hair and beard it framed. He was sitting beside Maruvka and at his feet lay a large hound.

'Ah, so you're here again?' began Bogratski. 'Do you seek revenge or are you ready to give in now?'

Sergei knelt before the lord and kissed his hand.

'That's right', said the latter. 'You shall remain here in the manor-house and do our bidding.'

Sergei rose and sighed.

'It amuses me', Bogratski stated, turning towards Maruvka, 'that your lover should become my lackey.'

'Me too', she replied, smiling. The chambermaid had just finished drying her feet. The hunting-dog had got up and began to lick her bare soles, but she drew her foot back suddenly and laughed out so loudly that the

"She looked a little pale, but a satisfied smile hovered upon her lips."

dog crawled quickly under the table. 'D'you know', she said then, 'that that is really a tremendously pleasant sensation—having the soles of your feet licked?'

She called the dog to her, but he would not come.

'What d'you want?' asked Bogratski.

'I want him to lick my feet.'

'But why should you need the dog for that?' exclaimed Bogratski with a devilish grin. 'That's just what this fellow's here for. Here, Sergei! Come! Do what the lady wants.'

'But, sir, I—I'm not a dog', stammered Sergei.

'We'll turn you into one', retorted Bogratski.

'Come here at once!' commanded Maruvka. Sergei did not budge; so Bogratski pulled him by the hair down to the floor, trampled him underfoot and lashed at him wildly with a dog-whip. 'Now will you obey?' he yelled as he struck him. 'Will you?'

Thus Sergei was brought into submission. He lay under Maruvka's feet and began to lick her soles; and when she had had enough, Bogratski made him pull off his own red morocco leather boots and perform the same servile function for him.

While Sergei like a dog, like a worm even, lay beneath his feet, he talked to Maruvka who was lounging lasciviously, resting her head upon his shoulder. 'This is a real delight, and the pleasure it gives me is doubled when I reflect that it is your erstwhile lover, that it is in fact my rival, who is obliged to provide it.'

A whole year had gone by. It was winter once more,— when suddenly, but not unexpectedly, the Polish Revolution of 1846 broke out. The ill-treated peasantry, instead of following the banner of the insurgents, turned their scythes and threshing-flails against them. Armed bands ganged together and made their way from manor-house to manor-house murdering all who fell into their hands. One such mob, led by Sergei, burst one morning into the manor-house of Bialagora. In vain did the defenders of the house shoot down a number of intruders: they broke in just the same and slew on the spot the officials and all the other employees.

Then Maruvka was dragged out of her hiding-place. The women ripped all her clothes from her body, tied straw round her middle and set fire to it. She rushed screaming through the village, pursued by a hail of flying missiles, until she collapsed and died at last, sprawled among a heap of hurled stones.

Bogratski's end was even more horrible. The peasants spread-eagled him with nails through his hands and feet, like a crucified vulture, to the barn-door and shot at him as a target for an hour or more with muskets and pistols. He had seven bullets in his body before they finished him off with their threshing-flails.

From the blood that flowed in streams that day this quiet, friendly country-seat thenceforward became known as "The Red Manor-House".

Today peace and harmony reign there.

The good old times have, thank heaven, vanished for ever.

THE WILD HUNTRESS

After the thirty years' war there took place in Bohemia a crude and barbaric deterioration of public morals that was truly incredible. The rich and powerful did as they pleased, with no fear that anyone would dare to call them to account. Law and justice were unknown concepts. One outburst of violence followed another, and the common people avenged themselves on the mighty by looting, murder and arson. All the restraining ties of discipline and order were torn to shreds by loftiest nobleman and humblest peasant alike.

It was only natural that in such circumstances even the character of the women became brutalised. They almost invariably actively associated themselves with whatever their menfolk did.

Among those women who became most feared and hated on account of their cruelty the Countess Vlasta Zesim took pride of place. She was a woman of thirty and possessed of exceptional beauty. Her husband was the commander of a cavalry regiment, and she had been with him in the war and shared with him all the rigours of military life; and when the Count, as the result of a bullet wound, became a cripple obliged to spend the rest of his life in an armchair, this woman, inured to a rugged wartime existence, could no longer confine herself to peaceable domesticity.

She owned a magnificent castle on the borders of the County Krumau. There she settled with her husband, and while he day-dreamed his life away between the four walls of his room, she thundered on racehorses over fields and woods or shot with a sure and practised hand at the wild animals which in the long years of her absence had enormously increased in numbers. Frequently she rode out at night to lie in wait for game or for poachers, and woe betide the unfortunate devil who fell into her hands! With fiendish pleasure she would have the poor wretch chased for hours on end by her hounds, and when he collapsed at last, all but torn to ribbons by the ferocious creatures, with savage delight she would plunge her long hunting-knife into his breast with her own hands.

She would arrange chases, to which she invited the horsemen from neighbouring estates, thus furnishing herself with opportunities to enable her to show off her great skill and daring before a circle of admiring spectators. Not one of the gentlemen could compare with her for cunning and audacity in pursuit of a wild animal: the consequence was that they all adored her and courted her good graces, but this wild Amazon was neither flirtatious nor sentimental. The tender expressions of love and the violent language of passion were alike completely alien to her heart, and a cooing suitor was in her eyes as laughable as he was contemptible.

For all that, she was very vain, exceedingly proud of her beauty, and once, when an admirer of hers, in a fit of pique at her frigidity, said he had seen a blacksmith's wife on the other side of the forest who was even much more beautiful than she, the Countess became consumed with fierce rage and made up her mind at once to exterminate this rival.

The next morning she halted at the door of the blacksmith's cottage which, to her chagrin, no longer stood within her territory and jurisdiction. She knocked loudly on the door, and as the married couple in fear and trembling hastened to attend her, she could not but admit to herself that this peasant woman really was much more beautiful than she. She was scarcely able to control her anger sufficiently to demand of the couple a glass of water, in order to provide a pretext for her summons. Nevertheless, when the blacksmith's wife brought her the water she asked for, her fury overwhelmed her and, with vicious hate, she dashed the contents of the brimming glass full into the giver's face, and as the shocked girl recoiled with a scream of terror, the Countess jabbed her spurs into her horse's flanks and rode off in a mad gallop.

After this she asked herself day and night how she could get this woman into her clutches in order to destroy her. Had the girl been one of her own vassals, she would readily have murdered her, but as it happened that the cottage lay outside her estate, she had no absolute right of life and death over the couple. At last she devised a plan and proceeded swiftly to its execution. The man, like all poor people in those days, was sure to be a poacher: all she had to do, then, was to catch him on her own domain, and once she had the man in her power the woman would no longer be able to elude her. She sent for her servants, therefore, and promised a sizable reward to anyone who should deliver the blacksmith to her, assuring them that he was the biggest and most dangerous of poachers and was wreaking the most shocking havoc in her forests. Vlasta's serving men, who were little better than a bunch of thieves, egged on by the proffered reward, in a very few days brought her the blacksmith bound hand and foot.

When the blacksmith's wife heard that her man had been captured, she went pale and trembling to the castle and flung herself at Vlasta's feet, pleading with her to spare his life. Vlasta feasted her eyes on this sight for some moments with fiendish satisfaction at the tricked girl's mortal terror. Then she began to bargain with her.

'What do you offer me if I give you your husband back alive?' she asked, observing the girl slyly.

'What can I possibly give you, my lady?' said the young woman sadly, and her dead drooped in dejection. 'I am very poor, as you know.'

'Sacrifice your beauty and I'll spare your husband's life.'

The young woman looked at her in astonishment. 'But how can I do that?' she asked.

'Tell me you are willing', answered Vlasta impatiently, and, so saying, she seized a flask that stood on a table before her, and before the wretched girl had time to reply, she tossed the fluid it contained right in that lovely face.

With a loud shriek of pain the girl sank to the floor, while Vlasta stood over her and with malignant curiosity watched the frightful work of destruction that she had brought about by means of the acid contents of the flask upon the features that only a few moments before had been so beautiful. As soon as the woman had convinced herself that her rival's beauty had been for ever destroyed, she let her go—without, however, allowing her captive husband to go with her.

The latter was yet to provide Vlasta with much enjoyment. She had promised his wife that she would not kill him, and that she did not do, but she was determined to have her fun with him still. She wrote to her hunting companions and invited them to come on a certain day and take part in a chase that she would specially arrange. When her guests were assembled, Vlasta made her appearance before them on horseback dressed in a red velvet riding-habit trimmed with marten-fur, and gave orders for the unlucky poacher, as was the custom at that time, to be bound to the back of a large powerful stag; then she had the gates of the castle courtyard thrown open, struck the stag a vigorous blow with her whip, and it fled through the courtyard gate in frenzied haste. When the animal had been given a slight start in the race, she ordered the pack to be let loose, and with much wild howling and yelping the hounds set off in pursuit of the stag. Then Vlasta made a sign to the meet to disperse and so the hunt was on.

Among the hunting-men was that same unrequited lover who had told her about the blacksmith's wife being more beautiful than she, and Vlasta had so contrived to arrange things that the hunted stag would be chased in the very direction where the poor woman's cottage stood. Before they reached the place, she called her admirer to her and asked him derisively:

'Isn't it somewhere near here where that famous beauty lives whom you once told me of?'

The horseman, overjoyed at having an opportunity to take the proud woman down a peg or two, immediately made haste to lead the way to the blacksmith's cottage. Vlasta gave orders for the stag to be driven in that direction; she herself hurried on in order to arrive, together with her admirer, at the same moment as the animal, so that she might enjoy the spectacle of the surprise on her escort's face. Both of them spurred on their horses and galloped wildly ahead of the others, slightly overtaking the pack, so as to draw up outside the cottage just a few seconds before it, and thus the hunted stag as it came up was to find itself trapped in a narrow circle by the beaters and the hounds.

At the sound of the shouting and baying of the new arrivals, the blacksmith's wife opened her door and came out. Vlasta anxiously watched the face of her suitor; evidently he no longer recognised the woman who before had been so beautiful. She asked him whether this must not be the one who called herself the blacksmith's wife.

At that moment the stag bearing the bleeding body of the unfortunate man reached the doorway of the cottage.

With a shriek that seemed to pierce the marrow of one's bones the martyred girl rushed to her helpless husband, and as she lifted his head and pressed it against her bosom, she uttered such a horrible blood-curdling curse against the perpetrator of this outrage that, strong as were Vlasta's nerves, she turned deathly pale, even to her lips, when she heard it. Quickly she turned her horse and bounded away.

Only now did Vlasta's admirers begin to grasp what must have gone before, and they recounted to the bystanders the probable sequence of events; and even if the listeners felt no pity, they were, to say the least, shocked at the manner in which this woman, so jealous of her beauty, had contrived to render her rival harmless.

The assembled company did not follow Vlasta home: she returned alone to her castle. In her rage at finding that her "joke" had miscarried, she struck a stable-boy who came to lead away her steaming horse so forcibly on the temple with the hard crop of her riding-whip that he fell dead immediately.

From that day forth Vlasta spent her life almost continuously in the saddle and in the forests. Day and night she rode hither and thither, coming home only occasionally at night to rest for a few hours and to change her clothes. People always called her now "The Wild Huntress" and kept well out of her way whenever they saw her from a distance.

Several years went by. One day, Vlasta was caught by surprise in a terrible thunderstorm in the middle of an open field. Well accustomed as she and her horse were to bad weather, even so she was obliged on this occasion to think about seeking shelter from the terrific lightning and thunder-claps. But before she could reach a place of refuge, a blinding flash rent the black sky, followed by an ear-splitting peal of thunder. Vlasta and her mount had no further need of shelter: the lightning had dealt them both a single deadly blow.

As chance would have it, the former suitor of the beautiful Countess, after the storm had abated, was riding across his fields in order to assess what damage had been sustained, when he happened to come upon the very place where "the wild huntress" lay buried beneath her horse, and so he was the first to see how the frightful curse had been fulfilled which the wife of the blacksmith had pronounced upon that cruel woman.

THE ATHALIAH* OF
ZLOTA REKA

Not far from the border of Bukovina, there lies on the steep banks of the wildly frothing Prut the sizable and wealthy township of Zlota Reka. Three edifices stand out: the manor-house, the lord of which in former times was the possessor of supreme authority and, virtually, of the village of Zlota Reka itself, but is today little more than the principal farmer hereabouts; the church, with its Greek-Catholic rectory buildings; and the so-called "holy palace", in which only a couple of years ago, reigned the female head of the mysterious sect of Dukhobortsi† that had strongly established itself in the village and indeed in the entire region. Her name was Kaschanka Kasvaya and she was referred to as "the Mother of God"; she ruled over the hearts and souls of the submissive believers like a thoroughgoing female despot.

The premises have something oriental about them. A tall fence completely enclosed the spacious residence and the administrative outbuildings. A strong door which, contrary to the normal Galician custom, was kept constantly shut, led to the main building. From outside there were no windows to be seen in the great house: they all looked on to a small garden surrounded by high walls,

* Athaliah: in the Bible, the evil daughter of Ahab and Jezebel who, in jealous rage, put to death all the children of the House of David, (except Joash who was successfully hidden from her). (2 Kings XI). Racine's greatest play, *Athalie*, treats of this theme.

† Dukhobortsi (commonly referred to as the Dukhobors): literally 'spirit-wrestlers', a sect of religious fanatics originating in Russia whence they were expelled, and dispersed, in about 1885. They practised mutilation (including castration), savage forms of flagellation, and evinced a sexual attitude towards women that to the non-believer is ambivalent and even contradictory.

and over this the huge leafy boughs of two gigantic lime-trees spread a dense and almost impenetrable green roof.

It was a Sunday and the strange "Holy Woman" of the Dukhobors had just held court and received her followers, when one of her most zealous disciples, Fedor Scherkevko, ushered into her presence a young and stately-looking couple.

Kaschanka Kasvaya sat, richly dressed and formally adorned, on a kind of throne. She was neither young nor beautiful, but nevertheless there was a certain fascination about her appearance that could not be gainsaid. Her formidable figure displayed a resilient buxomness, and her round, tanned face with its firm cheek-bones, small nose, and thick pouting lips, gave an impression of insatiable sensuality and brutal energy, such as frequently exert a magic spell over men. Only her great dark eyes were really beautiful, and they shone forth from under strong, bushy brows with almost diabolical shrewdness.

She surveyed the newcomers attentively. The man was a well-to-do young farmer from the neighbouring village of Sovisko. His name was Gregor Vartotchko and he was tall and slim, with a handsome, fresh face and luxuriant fair hair. His wife, Dada, was delicate and somewhat dispirited in appearance, almost too delicate for a peasant girl, pink and white, with thick black plaits and striking blue eyes. They both flung themselves face downward before Kaschanka and lay there prone, in motionless humility, while Scherkevko, who had greeted "the Mother of God" in similar manner, now on his knees addressed her concerning the young couple, whom he had newly converted.

Vartotchko and his wife had asked to be admitted into the Dukhobors' community, he said, and, in reply to Kaschanka's questioning, they affirmed that it was of their own free will that they wished to change their creed.

At a nod from Kaschanka, they both stood up, but only in order to approach her more closely, and thereupon fell on their knees again to kiss her feet, which were shod in high boots of blood-red morocco leather.

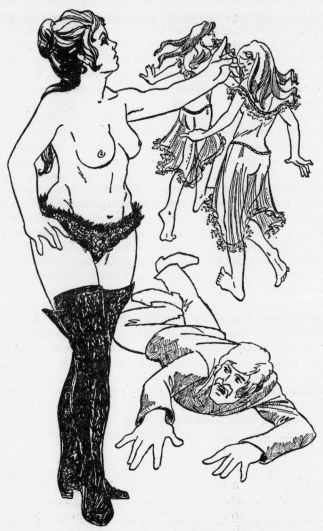

"... when she had sent the two maidens away, she began to enlighten Gregor ... as to the significance of this act of grace."

'I will arrange for you to be instructed in our Faith,' pronounced Kaschanka, 'and if, when you are sufficiently acquainted with our doctrines, you are still resolved to come over to us, we shall be happy to receive you with open arms and brotherly kisses. Stand up!'

Gregor and his wife rose, and stood aside, while different people, one after another, appeared before Kaschanka to present her with some request, or perhaps a gift, or to petition her judgment in some dispute.

While the arbiter was giving many proofs of her wisdom, her eyes continually strayed in the direction of the handsome farmer, and he in turn was contemplating her with similar constancy, though their thoughts were very different. Kaschanka was telling herself that Gregor showed promise of providing her with a very delightful pastime, but he, for his part, thought: 'So this is "the Saint!" She reminds me of our ageing milkmaid, except that this one's decked out more like a sleigh-horse.'

After that, the young couple were given instruction in the Dukhobor creed by two old men, and two weeks later were duly received into the community. The ceremony was reminiscent of the early days of Christianity. Both knelt before "the Mother of God", who bestowed on them the kiss of love; they then got up and were conducted round the circle of all the believers present, and each one greeted them with a low, truly oriental bow, followed by a brotherly or sisterly kiss.

To Gregor Vartotchko, however, only the antechamber of mystery had yet been unlocked.

Later the same evening two maidens, each crowned with a garland of roses, came to him and conducted him to Kaschanka's festively decorated boudoir. She herself was standing in the centre of it, and when she had sent the two maidens away, she began to enlighten Gregor, who had prostrated himself before her, as to the significance of this act of grace.

'It was through woman that Paradise was lost to man', she said. 'Therefore we Dukhobors believe that only

93

through woman can that lost Paradise be regained by mankind.'

Then she nodded to Gregor as a sign that he could get up,—and quickly clasped him to her breast . . .

He tried to break away from her, so she slapped his face hard and said:

'I happen to like you. And I propose, whenever I have time, to send for you.'

'That would be wrong', replied Gregor, taken aback.

'Will you explain yourself?'

'Is it not sinful for a married man to visit a strange woman in this way?'

'You don't understand.'

'If you command me, I will come', said Gregor, 'but I shall do so with a heavy heart.'

'Do you love your wife so much, then?' asked Kaschanka testily.

'How can I help loving a wife who is so young and beautiful?'

Kaschanka bit her lip.

'I gather you are a complete fool. See to it that you quickly improve. Out of my sight!'

Gregor went; he was glad to get away from her. For some time Kaschanka appeared to ignore him, but all the while in secret she was busying herself more and more with thinking about him. Until now, she was accustomed to regard all her followers as mere tools, or instruments, to satisfy her every whim, and had always found them ready, like slaves, to submit to her will. This was the first time she had met with opposition.

This angered her. She began to lust after Gregor.

One evening, she came unexpectedly to his cottage, ordered his wife to provide a meal, and then sent her away immediately, leaving Gregor to keep her company alone. However, later, when she began kissing him, he tolerated her love-making meekly, but with ill-concealed repugnance, like some misfortune one has to endure against one's will.

Suddenly, Kaschanka leapt to her feet.

'Do you imagine I've come here to bestow a favour on you that you by no means deserve? I'm only here to punish you for your sins. I look deep into your heart and I see how unclean it really is. On your knees! I will help you to do penance!'

He sank to his knees and she commanded him to sing the psalm of penitence; she seized him by the hair and smacked his face, and when, on her orders, he grovelled before her with his face in the dust, she trampled him underfoot and shouted at him: 'I'll make you mend your ways, you arrogant fool! You'll come crawling to me like a dog before I've done with you.'

Although her hatred, this savage fury of loathing that sprang from scorned love, had been allayed for the time being, her demoniacal longing to possess Gregor and to win his love increased in intensity day by day.

There were hussars in the village, and the officers were billeted at the manor-house. The latter were unutterably bored, and it so happened that one day the Captain of Horse, a sunburned Hungarian cavalier, was led by idle curiosity into the residence of "the Mother of God". One topic led to another, and finally Kaschanka, a mischievous smile on her sensual lips, asked playfully: 'Sir, what makes you complain that there's nothing to pass the time away with? There are some very pretty women here. Tomorrow evening, at supper time, you shall find one of the prettiest of them all, here with me.'

The next night the Captain of Horse duly returned, and sure enough there he found Gregor's wife Dada, whom Kaschanka had ordered by special messenger to be present. 'You now have an opportunity to prove that you have embraced our sacred doctrines with all your heart', said the female despot of the Dukhobors slyly to Dada. 'It will be your task to win this officer over to become one of us.'

The poor girl blushed crimson and protested, but it was of no use: Kaschanka commanded and threatened and at last Dada gave in, so that when the cavalry officer, without much ceremony, began to make love to her, he found her willing to be submissive and accommodating much more quickly than he had ever imagined would be possible.

A couple of months went by. Winter had come and Nature had proudly covered herself with a gleaming mantle of fleecy snow. Then one evening, a band of fanatical Dukhobors stormed into the village of Sovisko, thronged to Gregor's house and demanded with shouts of fury that the adulteress be delivered to them.

'Whom do you mean?' asked Gregor in astonishment.

'Your wife!' answered a hundred voices at once.

Poor Dada, in fear and trembling for her life, was dragged from the house. They stripped her, tied a girdle of straw around her middle and hung a heavy stone round her neck; then all the Dukhobors began to chant a pious hymn in chorus, and at the same time stones were hurled from all directions at Kaschanka's wretched victim.

In tears, Dada fled through the village, chased by the raging mob until she sank lifeless on the steps of the inn.

As in all such cases of peasant lynch-law, the subsequent investigation revealed nothing and the murderers went unpunished.

Some time after the death of Gregor's wife, Kaschanka came to Sovisko and called at Gregor's cottage. 'Now', she began scornfully, 'perhaps you can find time to spare some love for me?'

'I fear you', replied Gregor. 'More than that you cannot ask of me.'

'Then in future, at all events, you shall have good cause to tremble before me', cried Kaschanka. 'You, apparently, are not ready for me yet, but I'm certainly ready for you!'

The very next day, four Dukhobors brought the unfortunate Gregor, bound hand and foot, on a small sleigh to Zlota Reka. Kaschanka stood waiting for him outside her house, proud and forbidding, like an affronted tyrant.

Her dark complexion, contrasting with her flashing eyes and set off by the blood-red kerchief round her head, gave her a wild and gypsy-like appearance. She wore long red boots, and from shoulders to ankles was enveloped in a great black fur, on which the big red coral beads that she wore round her neck glowed like drops of blood.

At a sign from her, Gregor was hauled from the sleigh and taken into an empty barn; there he was brought to trial.

'Do you repent of your sin?' asked Kaschanka coldly.

'Which one? I have more than one sin on my conscience', replied the defendant.

'The sin against the love commandment, which you have transgressed.'

'Do you propose to punish me because you are not young and beautiful?' countered Gregor.

Now his doom was pronounced . . .

'You all hear how he blasphemes me!' said Kaschanka, her face distorted with fury. 'But you shall see how I will punish his blasphemy!'

They forced a crown of thorns on Gregor's brow and threw him face downward in a place strewn with thorn branches, and while the cruel spikes tore his face and body so that his warm blood dripped on the ground, four hefty men began to lash him with whips.

For a long time the scourged young man bore this incredible martyrdom with that stoic patience that distinguishes the Galician peasants, unflinching and without complaint. Kaschanka stood by, looking on with fiendish delight, and from time to time urged the Dukhobors not to slacken the force of their blows.

'Do you repent?' she asked at last. 'Do you promise to mend your ways?'

'Oh! Only now have the scales dropped from my eyes', answered Gregor, 'and I see you for what you are. You're no "Holy One", but the greatest sinner of all. You are the Athaliah of Zlota Reka!'

'This is apostasy!—the betrayal of our Faith!' burst out Kaschanka, grinding her teeth. 'This wretch, deluded by the Devil, is seeking to poison our whole devout community, to lead you into error and to do away with the eternal bliss of Paradise. He must die! Put him to death!'

She called upon two more fanatics to come and flog him with long whips, the thongs of which were weighted with lead. After a few strokes with these, this modern Athaliah's victim began to groan and finally to cry aloud.

While the Dukhobors chanted a penitential psalm, Kaschanka stood by motionless and without a word; on her sensual lips there played a horribly satisfied smile. Only when the poor martyr breathed his last sigh was her devilish lust for revenge appeased.

For yet one more year the strange "Holy Woman" of Zlota Reka continued to lead her outrageous existence unpunished.

Then another bloody crime was perpetrated, but this time the court managed to produce evidence that enabled it to bring accusations of homicide against Kaschanka Kasvaya and more than a score of her followers.

In one and the same night they were all arrested, clapped in irons and taken to the county jail.

Kaschanka was much too shrewd to have any doubts about her impending fate. After the very first interrogation she knew that she was lost.

She had a small flask of poison with her that she had concealed in her luxuriant hair.

One morning they found her dead, stretched out on her bunk.

Her disciples averred that she had been murdered in her prison cell, and even today she is still venerated as a martyr and a saint.

THE LADY WHO TAMED LIONS

It was at the beginning of the winter of 1859 that the famous Harsberg menagerie came to Bucharest for the first time. The whole town was filled with excitement by the very rare animals never before seen in such large numbers, by the beauty of the lion family, and even more by the lion-tamer herself who made the beasts perform the most incredible tricks.

She was a Swedish girl, called Irma Dahlstrem. She was beautiful, distinguished, fearless and—unapproachable. There was a rumour, it is true, that she was the beloved mistress of the menagerie proprietor, but the wealthy *boyars* who importuned her with their romantic attentions met with only a cold civility and an overweening pride which discouraged them from seeking to woo her.

She lived with the Harsberg family in the premier hotel of the town, drove like a great lady in their carriage to the menagerie and returned home in the same style, received no visitors, and never showed herself alone in the street or anywhere else. Such extreme reserve and vestal-like austerity tantalised the gallant gentlemen and aroused the curiosity of other people even more; and the Swedish girl soon became as popular in Bucharest as Catalani* and Lola Montez† had been before her.

One evening there came to the menagerie, fresh from a little escapade in Paris, Prince Maniascu, the darling of the ladies of Bucharest. Accompanied by some of his

* Angelica Catalani (1779-1849), Italian opera singer who made her début in Venice in 1797 and had a succession of triumphant appearances in almost every European country for over 30 years.

† Lola Montez (1818-1861), Irish dancer and adventuress notorious for her amorous *affaires* with Ludwig I of Bavaria and others.

friends, he inspected the different animals, took pleasure in watching them being fed and put through their paces, and finally stood before the lions' cage, a sceptical smile at his lips, to await the famous Swedish girl. Suddenly, at the back of the cage a narrow door opened and Irma made her appearance, to the accompaniment of frenzied applause. With an inimitably dignified movement she threw off the great velvety fur in which she was enveloped, and stood, all dressed in white satin and red velvet trimmed with ermine, nimble and smiling, into the cage, a wire whip in her hand, upright, svelte, with the noblest countenance in the world, to which luxuriant red-gold hair and a fresh complexion lent a truly fascinating charm. From the very first moment the Prince was ensnared: with mounting excitement he followed every movement, every accomplishment of her performance. His heart pounded as she thrust her lovely head into the fearful jaws of a lion, and a sweet shower of relief seemed to trickle over him whenever she addressed the fractious beasts with angry shouts or brought them under control with kicks and lashes of her whip.

Scarcely had the Swedish girl left the cage, when Prince Maniascu was already in her path; he stood directly before her, and—while she unhurriedly slipped into the fur which Edgar, the Harsbergs' extremely handsome son, held for her—she let her great blue eyes dwell with coy bewilderment, even with timidity, upon his perfect, almost femininely attractive features, and she answered his questions, not haughtily and coldly, as was her usual manner, but shyly and with an indescribably gracious smile.

The Prince now came night after night, and Irma not only welcomed him in the most affectionate manner, but even sought him out among the audience with a quick glance as soon as she entered the cage, and whenever the performance permitted kept her eye upon him, anxious to assure herself that he was still there. When she left the cage she would stamp her foot with impatience if he were not immediately on the spot to help her on with her fur. But that was all there was to it, for the Prince could get no further, and the more his bold persistence met with rebuffs, the more he became overwhelmed by a devilish desire to possess this intriguing woman entirely.

Unexpectedly a rival came to his aid. One evening, just before Irma stepped into the lions' cage, Edgar said to her with a quaking voice:

'I always thought until now that you were my father's mistress, and so I held my peace, but now I must tell you that I love you, and therefore I could never stand aside and say nothing while you throw yourself away on this *boyar* who is already engaged to a Princess and simply playing some dirty game with you.'

When the Prince came to her after the performance, she asked him point blank:

'Is it true that you have a fiancée?'

'It is true', replied the Prince, 'but any time you like that boring romance can be ended, and I will lie at your feet as your slave.'

'Ah! I don't believe you love me any more.'

'How can I prove to you that I do?'

She stared straight ahead of her. Then, in a low voice, she announced her sudden, bold decision. 'Come one hour before midnight to the little door behind the cage, which leads in to the menagerie.'

'I'll be there', was the answer.

And come indeed he did. As he left the menagerie in the darkness of the night, he was lovingly embraced by two soft arms and two burning lips glued themselves to his.

Soon in all the districts round about people were talking of the strange liaison between Maniascu and the beautiful lion-tamer. His father, concerned for his son's future, resolved to marry him as soon as possible to the Princess Agrafine Slobuda, to whom he had been betrothed from childhood. There was a stormy scene between father and son, but finally the Prince and the Princess were united and so there came an evening when he failed to appear at the menagerie.

That evening was followed, for Irma, by an excruciating night. Two more evenings came and went and she waited for her beloved in vain; then she wrote to him but received no answer.

On the fourth evening, as she left the cage and Edgar, with conscientious tenderness, wrapped her soft fur around her, he began: 'Irma, may I tell you why this scoundrel stays away?'

'Well?' she replied apathetically. 'I am prepared for the worst.'

'In three days he will celebrate his wedding.'

'You're lying!'

'Why should I lie?'

'What's the name of his bride?'

'Princess Agrafine Slobuda.'

'Is she pretty?'

'Pretty, young and rich.'

Irma uttered a shrill, venomous laugh.

'Just tell me that you will shed a tear for me, one solitary tear if I die for you', exclaimed Edgar, 'and you shall be avenged. I'll kill him . . . '

'No, Edgar, you must not sacrifice yourself, not you . . . '

'And so the swine shall go unpunished?'

'Certainly not', she answered with quiet resolution.

'Then let me kill him', murmured Edgar, his lips pale and quivering.

'No, said Irma, 'leave him to me.'

Edgar turned ashen grey as he looked into her devilish face, around which her red plaits, like fiery serpents, writhed and played. He said nothing.

The next afternoon, Prince Maniascu was sitting in the small, enchanting boudoir of his bride-to-be and rolling for her a cigarette in his well-manicured hands, when the Princess, with an arrogant and sardonic smile, expressed the wish to see, just once, this female lion-tamer whom everyone said was so remarkable.

'Whatever put such an idea into your head, Agrafine?'

said the Prince, while the cigarette-paper quivered in his hands and the golden tobacco flowed through his white fingers.

'Well, I have been told so many remarkable things about this person,' went on Agrafine slyly, 'that I have got it into my head that I must attend one of her performances, and indeed I want to go this very day and in your company, Prince.'

As the Swedish girl stepped into the lions' cage that evening, she caught sight of Maniascu and at his side a young and charming lady, who was surveying her challengingly through her lorgnette. This must be the Princess, his bride-to-be; she felt this immediately in her bones and quaked, but only for a moment; then she went into her routine with the wild animals as cold-bloodedly and intrepidly as ever. When, after a capital display of artistry, she reclined at full length on the back of the largest lion, while the others lay all round her, the Princess applauded loudly and tossed into the cage a purse filled with gold. An involuntary murmur ran through the tiers of spectators. Irma began to tremble, tears started from her eyes, she lost control of herself and over the animals that surrounded her; the huge lion raised his head, looked at her in astonishment, and suddenly seized her left arm between his terrifying teeth. A shriek of horror resounded from a hundred pairs of lips,—but Irma in that same moment had recovered herself. A single glance, a single word of command, and the lion had immediately let go of her arm. She now sprang up, seized the recalcitrant creature by the mane, placed her foot upon him and struck him with her brass-wire whip until he was again completely cowed and lay peacefully at her feet. Tumultuous applause and shouts of acclamation rewarded the courageous girl.

'When is his wedding?' she asked Edgar as soon as she had left the lions' cage.

'The day after tomorrow, Irma.'

'I want you to see that he gets a letter from me. Will you attend to it yourself?'

'Whenever you command.'

'I shall be most grateful.'

Irma shook his hand, but he seized hers and covered it with kisses.

The next morning the lion-tamer wrote to the Prince. Just once more she would like to see him and talk to him; she asked him to come at night to the menagerie at the usual hour, and promised that in return on his wedding-day she would leave Bucharest for ever. Edgar himself delivered the letter to the Prince. The latter perused it quickly, smiled and said:

'I'll be there.'

One hour before midnight the Prince appeared at the back-door of the menagerie. As usual it opened without difficulty. By the wan light of the stars and the snow Irma stood there in a short fur jacket, leaned towards him, took his hand and led him gingerly along the gloomy passage. As usual, a second door squeaked on its hinges, and the lion-tamer conducted the Prince through this into a completely dark room and here she flung her seductive arms around his neck and kissed him with wild abandon.

Then she suddenly disappeared; the door slammed shut and at the same moment the Prince's foot stumbled against something living, against something that began to move. What was this? Had she not, as always, led him into her dressing-room?

The next moment a harsh red light fell upon the scene. Irma had fixed a burning torch to an iron ring before the lions' cage, and in the centre of that cage, in the midst of the lions, was the Prince. He was petrified with fear. Irma who, her arms folded on her breast, was standing at the bars, stared at him with her cold blue eyes and uttered a short, satanic laugh. The Prince tried frantically to open the door, but in vain.

'For God's sake, Irma!' he implored her, 'what has come over you?'

'I am celebrating my marriage to you today and my lions shall be our guests.'

'Are you out of your mind?'

'I know perfectly well what I am doing. You have been a traitor to me and I have sentenced you to death. Forward, forward, my friends!'

She began to rouse and provoke the slumbering lions with her whip, while the Prince shouted for help. His cries, however, died away unheard in the winter storm. The lions, bewitched by Irma and incited by her loud shouts, pounced upon him. Soon his blood was flowing. He begged for mercy and tried desperately to defend himself, while she, her face pressed against the cold bars, feasted her eyes upon his mortal terror, upon his hideous sufferings.

It was a long time before the lions had accomplished their gruesome work. When the Prince lay dead, his tattered body strewn about the floor of the cage, the lions slunk away and began to lick their bloody paws.

That same night the beautiful lion-tamer disappeared from Bucharest and has never been heard of again.

KASIMIRA

Since time immemorial the beauty of Hungarian woman-
hood has played a primary role in the history of elegant
society in Greater Vienna. This is due to that particu-
larity of her race and her country that makes the
female Hungarian a composite of all the seductive qualities any single one of which would suffice to make her a
ravishing woman: passionate beauty, liveliness of spirit,
aptitude in public affairs, magnanimity, generosity, an
almost savage love of independence, the temperament of
an expert horsewoman, aristocratic pride, and a provokingly unpredictable attitude to the horizonal position.
In short, all the seductive qualities and faults that can
make a man extremely happy or extremely miserable.
A beautiful Hungarian woman will be the most virtuous
or the most maleficent of her sex, according to the environment in which her lot has chanced to throw her, and
depending upon the conditions of existence which destiny
has made for her, and the direction, good or evil, that
the influence of her surroundings has imprinted upon
this or that proclivity of her nature.

Kasimira, the chief character in this story, had, in essence, all that was needed to make of her either a Madonna
or an Astarte. If, very early in life, dark shadows got the
better of celestial influences, that was, perhaps, solely
because her family gave to her existence, from the beginning, a pernicious direction.

At the age of sixteen, they married her to an old man,
whom she could not love or esteem and who was capable
of instilling into her nothing but fear. She was of noble
birth, but poor. In order not to let her fall further from

her rank, her family felt that they must, at all costs, make sure she contracted a wealthy marriage.

The consequences of this misguided calculation were what they nearly always turn out to be. When parents, in the belief that they are doing the right thing, trample underfoot some ideal that lies latent in the heart of their child they cause, more often than not, to germinate in its place disillusionment, hatred, vice; it is fortunate indeed if the existence thus turned awry does not degrade into a life of crime, instead of one of calm content and universal respect.

Kasimira's character and temperament were not such as would let her become resigned to her fate and suffer in silence. Her austere and joyless marriage soon made of this precocious, passionate young girl a bizarre and capricious woman, forthright, wayward and proud. She quickly acquired the habit of seeking, outside, the satisfactions that were denied her at home. But she was obliged to use a great deal of prudence so as not to arouse the jealousy of her aged husband, whose temper was choleric and vindictive; above all, she was concerned to preserve the Asiatic luxury and splendour by which she was surrounded. The need to dissimulate and to restrain herself made her every day more cunning, more eager for pleasures, more depraved.

Kasimira was one of that wild race of women who have played a typical role in the history and the legends of Hungary; one of those women, who, to preserve perpetual freshness and youth, to remain ever beautiful, did not shrink from bathing in human blood, who harnessed their lovers to a plough and belaboured them with lashes of the whip, or who had them sewn into the skins of bears and then let loose upon them packs of ferocious hounds.

This woman was possessed of a devilish beauty. Her tall, slim figure revealed with every movement the litheness, the elasticity and the energy of the feline race, at once so graceful and so cruel. Hair black as a raven's wing and unusually abundant framed her enchanting face, the somewhat dusky shade of which, delicately tinted with rouge, was redolent of the Orient. Beneath the mysterious veil of long black lashes blazed two large, inscrutable eyes.

As a horsewoman, Kasimira, by dint of her daring and bewitching gracefulness, attracted general attention, not only in Vienna, but also in the land of her birth, where she resided throughout the summer, moving from one of her estates to another, arousing the admiration of the women as much as the men's. Whoever found himself in her presence, drawn into her enchanting inner circle, could not fail to feel at once the magnetic power of that queenly nature, which no one could ever resist. People vied with each other in submitting to her with alacrity and enthusiasm; yet, in the midst of that circle over which she reigned as undisputed sovereign surrounded by her subjects, she often showed herself to be more imperious and more heartless than the most abominable despot.

In Vienna, she was constrained to bridle the passions of a Centauress; but a ride in the Prater or the Ringstrasse was far from satisfying to this tireless horse-breaker.

Just the same, she had to be content with it. The theatre, gambling, meetings, reading, the voluptuous desires that she herself purposefully aroused among the host of men who paid their attentions to her, occupied the greater part of her time. To make up, in summer, when she was re-installed in her ancient feudal castle, she ceaselessly traversed the vast plains, sometimes on horseback, sometimes driving her four-in-hand herself, in the manner of a Trojan hero. Or, again, she would amuse herself by reducing some poor fox to desperate extremities, or hunting an unfortunate hare without mercy, accompanied by a train of handsome men and women devotees, who egged each other on to jump the hedges and ditches, and even the most dangerous obstacles, ahead of her, indifferent though she was whether they fell or not: indeed, she could not have cared less if they broke an arm, a leg, or even their neck.

As often happens amongst the Hungarian nobility, her husband had generously undertaken to pay for the studies of the son of one of his minor employees, a youth who had been orphaned while still young and who showed a great deal of intelligence.

This boy's name was Stefan Bakaczi. He was placed at first in the college of a small town in a distant part of Hungary. Later, the magnate sent for him to come and live with him in Vienna, in order to finish his studies at the University. The first impression that Stefan made on the patron and his young wife was so favourable that it was resolved to treat him as the son of the house.

Stefan was now a good-looking fellow of twenty, well-built, fresh, with a peaches-and-cream complexion like a young girl's. In his blue eyes one could detect, at the same time, a certain simplicity and noble enthusiasm. He was rather shy and awkward, but Kasimira took it upon herself to educate him and bring him out: this would give her something amusing to do. And indeed, before he had been under the young woman's tuition for six months, the intelligent student had already acquired all the distinction appropriate to an aristocrat.

In the month of May, the husband and wife went away, as they did every year, to spend the summer on their estates in Hungary, and Stefan remained behind almost alone in Vienna, accompanied only by the steward, to continue his studies there. With the advent of the summer vacation, he went off to join his patrons.

By an unfortunate mischance, Kasimira was alone in the castle. Her husband, who took a great interest in politics, had gone to Pest. In his absence, the young wife, greedy for conquests and pleasure, was more than ever condemned to exercise restraint, for she was in no doubt that her husband had her constantly spied upon. She received no one, found life immensely monotonous, and was terribly bored.

Stefan's arrival, giving promise of providing a pastime and a welcome change, was therefore quite an event for her. She went to meet him at the nearest railway station and brought him back to the castle, driving the carriage-and-four herself.

Until now, Stefan had had no relations with the magnate's beautiful wife, except of the most formal kind in the presence of her husband and of the strangers who came and went at the Palace; now he would have to live virtually face to face with this passionate woman, who had too much time on her hands, yet was condemned to be careful and secretive.

Kasimira had simply nothing to do, and she wanted to amuse herself at any price. She began to flirt with the young man, giving no thought whatever to anything that lay beyond. But something happened which she may or may not have dreamed of. Shy, innocent, without experience of life, completely nurtured on illusions, Stefan took very seriously what was merely a game to the idle beauty, and, after a few days, fell madly in love. When Kasimira realised the depth and purity of the passion she had so imprudently inspired, she gave herself up uninhibitedly to all her instincts, and began to make love to the poor student in her own bizarre fashion, trying out on him the most eccentric whims and fancies, and now and then the cruellest that came into her mind. She tormented him incessantly in every imaginable way. One day, she poured beer into his wine, and made him drink this infernal mixture to the last drop. On another occasion, she ordered his chambermaid to put stinging-nettles in his bed.

All at once, the idea occurred to her of making him ride a horse. The unfortunate disciple of Horace and Virgil protested in vain that equitation was something he had never tried: he was obliged to follow Kasimira to the riding-stables, where she herself took on the job of giving him instruction.

It was a comic but at the same time a cruel scene. At every moment, the poor devil would let go of the reins to cling like grim death to the mane of his mount, while his implacable mistress, standing in the centre of the exercise yard, a cigarette between her lips, continuously urged on the horse with resounding blows of the whip. Stefan fell off several times, but he always remounted, stimulated by the laughs and jeers of his tyrannical instructress and in spite of the bruising of his arms and legs.

But this barbarous amusement was far from satisfying the cruel instincts of the Amazon; in order to compel her wretched admirer to remain on the horse, she had recourse to a drastic means, much employed in Hungary: she had him tied by the knees to the stirrups, leapt into the saddle herself, and seizing the bridle-rein of Stefan's horse, galloped off across the plain carrying her poor victim away with her.

After a wild career lasting more than an hour, she brought the young man back to the castle, more dead than alive. When he had been untied, he was incapable of getting off the horse by himself: the grooms had to carry him in their arms to his bedroom. Far from showing the slightest pity, Kasimira only joked and scoffed at her guileless laughing-stock.

Lying prone on a shabby old sofa, all his limbs racked with pain, the unlucky young man cudgelled his brains in trying to understand what he could have done to have aroused so much aversion in the woman whom he loved so dearly, for the disdainful and heartless way she had been treating him for some time could surely only be inspired by loathing. Meanwhile, something happened that Stefan would never had dared to hope for. Kasimira came into his room, sat at his bedside, evinced great compassion for him, and chatted with him in a more amiable way than he had ever known before.

He was at once astonished and delighted. However, this was not all. Suddenly, this woman, so haughty, so beautiful, took Stefan's head in her arms and covered it with kisses. Moved to the depths of his soul, thrilled, enraptured, the poor young fellow abruptly forgot his sufferings and the mad chase that had caused them; even forgot the still more cruel sneering of this woman, whom he worshipped; he flung himself on his knees, clasped her in his arms, which she had tortured so, faltered the tenderest words of love to her, told her all that he felt with a wealth of sentiment and eloquence of expression of which he could not have believed himself capable a few minutes earlier.

That same night, Kasimira was his,—or rather he was hers; for this woman never gave herself completely: she would throw her arms with furious passion around the man she happened to love at the moment, only to repulse him scornfully as soon as she wanted him no longer.

So, he was hers, and, from that day on, the ancient castle, not long ago solitary and deserted, all at once seemed peopled by a host of joyous little spirits and roguish cupids, who made of it a love-nest garlanded with roses.

Unfortunately, this ecstatic idyll was destined to be of short duration. It was not long before the old magnate returned; and after that the two lovers were almost entirely deprived of their delightful intimacies.

But Kasimira's character was not the sort that would put up with such restraint indefinitely. While her husband was playing chess with Stefan, she would spend whole hours plunged in reverie, reclining on a divan, or else would mount a horse and dash off across the plains, covering vast distances, her hair unbound and swept this way and that by the wind.

Whatever she did, at home or in the open steppe, she felt vaguely asserting themselves in her brain, like so many demons, a host of evil thoughts. It was mere chance that revealed to her what was going on inside her, what she had for long ardently desired without really knowing it.

At that time brigandage was flourishing in Hungary. Not a day passed but one would hear of some grave and daring robbery, or some hideous assassination. The government had proclaimed martial law: military patrols swept the country continually, the gibbets were never idle. Nevertheless, these repressive measures, inexorable though they were, brought no relief from the lamentable situation.

In accordance with the prevalent custom, Kasimira's husband concluded a kind of conditional treaty with the brigands, by which he undertook to furnish them regularly with a specific sum of money and to entertain them in princely fashion whenever they came to his place and demanded hospitality. In return for these services, the magnate and his staff were assured against all attack, against any murder and any depredation on the part of the brigands.

One fine day, the brigands gave notice of their impending visit. Preparations were duly made to provide them with good cheer and entertainment. Casks of old wines were brought up from the cellars, gypsy musicians and girls were engaged for their pleasure. In due course the brigands dropped in, made free with abundance of food and drink, and gave themselves up to merry-making to their hearts' content. They were in the act of dancing gaily to the strains of a *czardas** when one of their lookouts suddenly came rushing in to announce that the dragoons were coming.

In the twinkling of an eye, they made for their horses, ready saddled beforehand, spurred their mounts furiously and turned their backs abruptly, so to speak, on the envoys of the King.

The lord of the manor was keenly upset by this incident: the brigands, he thought, would be bound to assume that he had betrayed them and would take revenge upon him!

When he was expressing these apprehensions to Kasimira, it came to her like a bolt from the blue that never would a finer opportunity present itself to enable her to gain her independence, while continuing to live in regal opulence.

Obsessed by this criminal notion, which caused her to cast aside all discretion, when night came she went to rejoin her young lover. Locked in his tight embrace and intoxicated by caresses, she revealed to Stefan her diabolical plan. The young man was shocked by it and urged her to give up the abominable scheme. But she invoked

---

* Czardas: Hungarian dance in two movements, one slow and the other very fast.

the love, the great passion, that he, Stefan, had aroused in her, tantalised him with glimpses of the unclouded bliss that awaited them, once they were both free, and basking in the lap of luxury and riches; she was, by turns, suppliant and menacing, and ended by leaving her lover to choose between losing possession of her and participating in a crime.

When she had left him, Stefan, distracted with voluptuousness, and whom the very thought of giving up his superb mistress had made cowardly and vile, was resolved to go the lengths of the most heinous of crimes: he would kill his benefactor, or cause him to be killed.

A few days later, the magnate was obliged to go and visit one of his neighbours to negotiate with him the purchase of a forest. He left alone, on horseback, early in the morning. He was due to return the same afternoon. The following day he had still not re-appeared!

Kasimira then ordered her horse to be saddled and, accompanied by a few of her servants, set out to search and scour the neighbourhood in quest of her husband. At last, he was discovered lying in a pool of blood in a ditch beside the highway: he had been assassinated and robbed.

Kasimira leapt from her horse and flung herself upon the corpse of the rich man, her late husband, uttering heart-rending lamentations. Half-fainting, she had to be carried back to the castle.

All the enquiries that were made to discover the assassin were in vain. The conviction remained that the crime was the work of the brigands who had thus taken their revenge for the lord of the manor's alleged betrayal.

But one day, the Chief of Security received a note written in dog Latin, in which he was assured, in the name of the brigands, that not one of them was guilty of this murder gratuitously laid to their charge, and that what they would advise him to do was look for the author of the crime in the magnate's "immediate *entourage*".

The Magistrate went at once to the castle with a view to questioning the staff.

Completely self-controlled, though ostensibly a prey to the keenest affliction, Kasimira, in response to the Magistrate's interrogation, affirmed that she had no suspicions concerning those around her but that, on the contrary, she was absolutely certain that the murder of the late magnate, her husband, was an act of vengeance perpetrated by the brigands.

Even so, like a conscientious civic officer, the Chief of Security set to work at his duty of interrogating meticulously all the occupants of the castle, one after the other. The outcome of this inquest was fruitless. The Magistrate was convinced that none of the persons whom he had interviewed was implicated in the magnate's assassination.

Stefan was at that time absent from the castle.

As the Magistrate was going away, followed by his *pandours*, Stefan, returning suddenly, came face to face with him in the castle courtyard. The young student immediately turned pale at the sight of the Magistrate who, however, had cast only a casual glance in his direction. At once, a terrible suspicion leapt into the mind of the Security inspector: he set about questioning the new arrival forthwith and gave orders to his escort to defer the departure.

Stefan was confused and his replies seemed so embarrassed, so incoherent, that in the end he was arrested and held in custody. One hour later, left with not a leg to stand on, he confessed his dastardly and abominable crime. And so, as he stubbornly insisted that he had had no accomplice, he was summarily tried and sentenced to be hanged that very day.

As they were laying hold of the poor wretch and tying his hands behind his back, he started trembling all over, and, staring hard at the castle of his benefactor, began to sob and shed burning tears. Then, in the midst of his anguish, he perceived, at one of the castle windows, the despicable woman, whose diabolical influence had made of him—simple, honest soul—an odious felon.

The lovely female monster never flinched; she met his gaze steadily and showed not the slightest emotion. A few moments later, poor Stefan's body was swinging lifeless on the gallows.

This terrible event did not prevent Kasimira from betaking herself that very day to a Bohemian spa. In the midst of the glamorous pleasures of high society in that enchanting place, she soon managed to forget the outraged shades of her husband and her lover. The following winter, she was to be seen in Paris in the company of a handsome and elegant Pole, who, since he had no means of support of any kind, was clearly nothing but an unprincipled adventurer. Then she went off to Vienna, where, in obedience to the impetuosity of her passionate desires, she gave herself up to the vilest orgies.

Several years went by, and then in Baden a woman, prematurely aged, her face as evil as a vampire's and her eyes dull and lifeless, could be seen being pushed about in a bath-chair. Everyone kept out of her way and avoided speaking to her. She was paralysed and only with difficulty could she make herself understood by signs to an old servant who wheeled her bath-chair here and there in the park.

This was that same woman who, once upon a time, had been the lovely and joyous horsewoman: Kasimira. . .

Now she was having to endure the punishment she deserved for her bloody deeds!

THE FEMALE HYENA
of the HUNGARIAN PLAIN

Chapter I

TEMPTATION

In Vienna, one fine Winter's day, the great ladies of quality, comfortably wrapped in their expensive furs, sauntered along the Ringstrasse, while the poor, ill-clad working women trembled with cold as they made their way from their garret homes to their work and back again.

Towards evening, just as the displays in the different shop windows of the Graben began to glitter in the gaslight, there chanced to pass that way a beautiful girl who attracted the attention of the male passers-by: they vied with each other in casting flirtatious glances in her direction.

This girl seemed not only poor but even to be in the throes of a fiercely peevish melancholy: she seemed acutely aware of her indigence, to deplore her lot, and appeared as though she were beset by an uncontrollable yearning for luxury in singular contrast to the wretched rags that covered her and were totally inadequate to protect her from the cold.

Shivering all over, her cheeks pale and numb, her lips drawn, she stopped to look in the window of a dress shop, the wonders of which caused her heart to pound with covetousness, just as if she had been herself a lady of quality.

Her eyes burned with profound attention as they wandered ceaselessly, now over costly silk gowns or silken shawls, now over a skirt of a black lacy material or another trimmed with ermine and surmounted by a white fur jacket for the theatre.

As the poor girl gazed in astonishment at all these marvellous things, her sad face became contorted and took on an expression of mingled hate and envy, and she murmured inaudible words, railing against the Creator for having made such a lovely world, only to populate it with unhappy and poverty-stricken people.

Yet, at the very moment when some half-submerged diabolical trait in her nature was making itself felt she looked more beautiful and more desirable than ever.

Such, evidently, was the opinion of the handsome and elegant young man who, with a fortuitous glance, had caught sight of her profile; as if bewitched by her magic charms, he stood beside her, pretending to be studying the latest fashions but in reality concentrating all his attention upon his fascinating neighbour.

When at last she moved away, the young man followed her, and as they came to a dark, secluded spot near the Town Hall, he raised his hat and asked her to condescend to let him walk with her.

The beautiful and strange young girl gave him a withering look, then walked on without a word.

'My request was not meant to be offensive and is not one of those propositions made so frequently to women in Vienna at this time of day', said the stranger when he caught up with the girl again. 'Please permit me to say that the way you were standing just now looking at that gleaming display of fashions in that shop in the Graben filled me with the liveliest interest in you.

'You seemed to me to be possessed of a passionate love of luxury and splendour and yet, in spite of that, to be poor. Your good taste and your extraordinary beauty raise you above any princess or countess in our society, and that you remain poor presents me with a puzzle the only solution to which must lie in the fact that you are honest.'

'You are right, sir', replied the beautiful but shabbily dressed girl. 'I am poor,—but good.'

'I'm glad to hear it. That only increases the interest you inspire in me', answered the stranger, 'and I should be delighted if you would condescend to allow me to provide you with the luxury enjoyed by wealthy women and fallen girls.'

'How could that be?' said the girl naïvely.

'Men of my rank and station show total lack of restraint where women of the theatre and other naughty kinds of modern Messalinas are concerned: for their sakes they will dissipate their fortunes, become their slaves, sometimes even forfeit their lives, and in return these women make fools of them and when the unfortunate fellows are ruined their wretched mistresses trample them pitilessly underfoot.

'For my part, I have no taste for those kinds of women. My ideal is simply to find some sweet and honest working-class girl who is healthy in mind and body.'

'You can pick one up out of the muck and slime where such creatures are so comfortably at home!' said the girl in a tone that was almost violent.

'You misjudge me', replied the stranger in a calm, distinguished voice. 'I do beg you not to pursue this attitude any further, but to do me the small favour of providing me with an opportunity of getting to know you better, and of taking a little trouble yourself to understand my point of view. Please be assured that you are dealing with a man of honour. Here is my card. My name is Jules, Baron Steinfeld.'

The girl took the card and said nothing.

'You will not deign to answer me?' asked Baron Steinfeld.

'I'll talk to my parents about it', she said. 'For today you must be satisfied to know only that my name is Anna Klauer; my father is a factory worker, my mother is a washerwoman, and I myself am a glove-maker. Tomorrow, at about this time, be at the foot of the Town Hall tower: I'll give you my answer then.'

So saying, with a slight toss of her head she went away, with as much assurance in her step as any real princess, while the Baron, removing his hat and bowing till it all but touched the ground, remained rooted to the spot and followed her with his eyes as long as he could.

The next evening the Baron was more than punctual at the rendezvous, but the lovely glove-maker kept him waiting. As she approached, he rushed impatiently to meet her. At this the girl laughed to herself involuntarily: she was flattered to see this grand gentleman of quality so impassioned on her account.

'All my happiness, I swear to you', said the Baron, who sounded moved, 'at this moment hangs upon your lips! Speak, I beg you!'

'You exaggerate', she said, and at once her face took on a serious, even harsh, expression.

'I speak the truth, Anna', murmured the Baron, seizing her poor little hand that was quite blue and numb with cold, 'for I am in love with you already: yes, from the moment I set eyes on you I have worshipped you. But what's this? your hands are like ice! Can it be that you're ill? Won't you let me protect your darling hands from the cruel cold nip in the air?'

'How so?' said Anna innocently, and meanwhile the Baron, by a subtle détour, was leading her, almost without her realising it, back into the centre of town. And there they went.

'And you will not demand anything afterwards if I let you take me?' this poverty-stricken young girl asked of the smartly-dressed young man with a haughty tilt of her head.

'I ask it as a favour. Take as long as you possibly can to let me know your decision if it must be to rob me of that divine pleasure that I had hoped for!'

Anna began to laugh.

'Tell me I may accompany you!'

'What makes you think you may?'

'Your dear, good, beautiful eyes say it for you. Oh, what superb eyes you have, Anna!'

'All right. You may come with me,—on condition that you promise to respect me.'

'I give you my word as a gentleman!' exclaimed Baron Steinfeld. At the same time, he offered Anna his arm and she took it without demur. Seeing him walking quite openly beside her through the brilliantly lighted streets restored her confidence, and she was quick to see the advantages of the situation.

She sensed that this kind of intimacy imposed upon the Baron vis-à-vis herself obligations of a very different nature from those that generally unite a rich gentleman and his mistress, at whose feet he may be willing enough to throw himself in the privacy of the bedroom, but whom he could not bring himself to recognise on the open street. Her reasoning was in this respect quite incontrovertible.

Even so, on the Graben, something happened that threw the poor working girl completely off balance: Baron Steinfeld quite unexpectedly opened the door of a furrier's and before Anna Klauer had had time to realise what was taking place she found herself all at once among princely ermines and sables, being humbly invited by her companion to choose something for herself.

She was flabbergasted; the blood went to her head, and there was a jangling in her ears like a full peal of bells; momentarily she found herself entirely at a loss for words. A friendly assistant came to her rescue, and she was brought a costly jacket of black velvet trimmed and lined with golden sable; in the twinkling of an eye a stylish fur toque adorned her simple black curls, and in a trice her hands were nestling in the soft protection of a thick fur muff.

So overcome that she felt more dead than alive, she left the shop, and it was only when she was in the street once more that she recovered her speech. She turned to the Baron intending to reproach him, to reprimand him, —but she couldn't!

The regal furs had tamed her haughty spirit. The Baron did not fail to notice the change his master-stroke had wrought in the beautiful young girl; however, he was shrewd enough to content himself on this occasion with simply accompanying her to her home.

He took his leave of her by blowing her a kiss, and it was she herself who, before she went up the stairs, reminded him of his promise to come and see her again.

The following day, a liveried lackey brought the little

glove-maker a love-letter from the Baron, couched in the most fervent terms, and accompanied by a casket containing a jewel of great price. Anna was dazzled, confused, utterly fascinated; and when, towards evening, the Baron paid her a visit, she who had formerly been so proud, could not find words to express her gratitude.

The young gentleman did not stay long in the humble dwelling of these poor people. He left, soon afterwards to be followed by two footmen who took from a large hamper a good supper and several bottles of best vintage wines, all of which they placed on the table, and then withdrew.

The factory hand, and his wife the washerwoman, toasted the good cheer that had thus fortuitously come their way and emptied a number of bottles in drinking the Baron's health; as for the girl, she was deep in thought, melancholy almost.

She felt she had already gone too far, that now she could not stop herself, and suddenly the spirit of this proud, headstrong, imperious being, born to have men prostrate themselves at her feet and not to become their plaything, was as it were invaded by vexation and felt itself outraged.

The Baron was most zealous in appearing not to notice Anna's strange mood, and when, as he was leaving her a trifle late, Anna was lighting his way out from the top of the stairs, he removed his hat and bowed very low, offering the beautiful girl his very kindest regards in a most courteous but cold manner.

But now that the Baron seemed no longer to be entreating her, she suddenly felt free, and, overcome with emotion, threw herself into the arms of the handsome and elegant young man. She drew him back, put out the light, and in the darkness held him in her arms and furtively placed on his lips a kiss that was full of feminine seductiveness.

Then, like a frightened doe she fled, and rushed upstairs.

Chapter II

The old, old Story

More than two months had gone by since Baron Steinfeld had first met Anna Klauer, and still he had not succeeded in winning the beautiful girl to his will. She for her part accepted his costly gifts with ingenuous delight; he continued to shower them upon her, and seemed to think himself amply rewarded if she allowed him to kiss her with burning lips or merely shake her hand.

Unfortunately for him, it happened that the wealthy aristocrat who so magnificently adorned his needy victim whose intoxicating beauty now surpassed by far that of the great ladies in the land, was now permanently in the grip of a mounting passion and yet still could not bring himself to put to the object of his desire the fatal question.

Yet it was not that he had less admiration for her virtue than for her pride, not to say for that certain something which often enables the worst of women to subjugate the most intelligent of men and to overawe him to such an extent that, as was the case with the Baron, he finds himself involved in a love affair in a manner worthy of some enthusiastic but inexperienced schoolboy.

Then, out of the blue, an ally supervened from whom he had least expected support. The girl's parents on whose minds the Baron's first visit had left an indelibly bright impression, began to fear thereafter that Anna's scorn might reach the point of discouraging their distinguished visitor, and that consideration decided them without more ado to sacrifice their daughter's virtue to their own well-being.

Thereupon they set about tormenting the proud girl in every conceivable way until they convinced her that she was trampling all her happiness underfoot.

One morning, when the Baron had just finished breakfast, he was sitting in an armchair in his elegant town house, wearing a violet-blue dressing-gown and with a fez perched on his head; he was smoking a long Turkish pipe which, in view of his attire, gave him the appearance of a Pasha.

He puffed out the smoke to right and left which, as it rose in the air, formed itself into innumerable spirals and bizarre shapes; however, the Baron had thoughts only for the platonic odalisque, the beautiful Anna.

Suddenly, he heard what sounded like the rustle of a woman's skirts, and as he quickly turned his head he saw Anna Klauer in person standing there before him. It was the first time she had ever crossed the threshold of his home.

Something extraordinary must have happened, all the more so because on this occasion she had taken the trouble to cover her face with a thick veil. As she uncovered her features, the Baron looked at her in surprise; like a great lady to the manner born she returned his gaze.

Around her slim, well-formed figure fell the long majestic pleats of a black velvet gown, while a half-open jacket of the same material bordered with costly sable partially revealed the superb contours of a young girl's breasts. A black velvet hat trimmed with a long white feather completed her outfit. One of her finely gloved hands held a muff which was of sable too.

And now as she paced quickly to and fro in the room he was able to catch a glimpse from time to time of a delightful little foot shod in boots of black velvet enhanced with narrow bands of sable fur.

For some time neither of them uttered a word. Both the rich aristocrat and the poor working girl felt that the two of them had reached a grave and dangerous crisis in their lives.

Steinfeld was the first to break the silence, after he had stood up and offered Anna an armchair.

'What is it you want of me, Anna dear?' he said. 'Your visit almost alarms me.'

'My visit alarms you?' exclaimed the beautiful girl in a tone that sounded almost incensed. 'You still love me, don't you? Haven't you sworn that you do more than a hundred times? Or is it that you don't love me any more? Speak!' She stamped her foot with impatience.

'Do I love you!' replied the Baron, going up to her. 'Why, I adore you, and I have no other desire than to be your slave for ever!'

He knelt before her and pressed her hand to his ardent lips.

Anna surveyed him with a long, strange look.

'Today your desire shall be fulfilled', said the beautiful woman at last. 'I want to be your—your mistress. As the French say, your *maîtresse.*'

As she said this she gave a little burst of laughter that sounded sinister.

'I don't understand you, Anna,' replied the Baron, still at her feet.

'You certainly will understand me', said the beautiful girl. 'For a long time my parents have been reproaching me for living on them instead of giving myself to a rich admirer. Today they threatened to turn me out of the house unless I heeded them.

'As far as I'm concerned, and please get this quite straight, I am much too proud to make any such bargain: I threw at my parents' feet the diamonds you have given me; now I'm out of their debt, and I have left their home for ever.

'I have come to you because . . . '—she stopped, tears stifling her voice—'because I . . . I love you. I belong to you. Take me whenever you wish,—if you still love *me!* . . .'

'Great God!' exclaimed Steinfeld. 'Today you have made me the happiest of mortals.'

He rose to his feet and clasped the beautiful and superb young woman in his arms in an ecstasy of tenderness.

She remained silent, incapable of any act of will. He carried her to a couch, took off her hat, tossing it into the nearest corner, let down her delightful hair, and then, inflamed with passionate desire, tore away the fur that covered her delectable breast . . .

She gave herself to him.

That very same day he chose for her, in the Ringstrasse, an apartment furnished with all the refinements of luxury. The poor working girl thereafter lay between damask sheets and covered with eiderdowns embroidered with Brussels lace; every morning from then on, when she got up, wearing only gold-trimmed slippers and with a majestic (if not royal) bath-robe lightly clinging to her lovely body, her dainty feet would sink into a Persian carpet; and if you had happened to be in her box at the Opera you would have seen a thousand diamonds glittering and sparkling at her neck, on her head, or gracing her ears.

The Baron had become her slave: whatever she demanded of him he carried out with pleasure. When her humour so decreed, he would lie at her feet like a slave . . . , like a dog!

Now the parents of the beautiful girl sought to become reconciled to her. Every time they came to see her she had them shown off the premises by the servants. And so things went on for two years.

From the beginning of the third year her admirer became more and more cold towards her. He undertook the social obligations that his great name imposed, and at last he confessed to his paramour that his family wished him to marry.

One evening, Anna, having gone to the Opera but with no thought of meeting him there, saw him in the company of two ladies. She learned that one of them,—the younger one, a fragile, almost puny young blonde—was his fiancée; what was more, a lady sitting near her apprised her of the fact that the person in question was a certain Countess Thurn and was endowed with an enormous fortune.

Anna had heard enough. Before the next Act began, she left the theatre.

When the performance was over, the Baron came, as if nothing had happened, to take tea with Anna.

She looked him up and down in a most sinister manner.

'You show very good taste, I must say, to come and seek *me* out now of all times, considering you have just left your beloved, your fiancée! Make up your mind between her and me!'

'Who told you this?' said Baron Steinfeld, his cheeks red as fire.

'Don't try to lie to me. I saw you myself right beside her', said she as cold as steel.

'So you spy on me now!' he exclaimed. 'You follow me about and lurk in my path to compromise me, do you?'

'I should think that up to now if anyone has compromised anyone, it's you, you wretch!' she said fiercely.

'Did you not come to me of your own free will?' asked the Baron by way of reply. 'Did you not offer yourself? If I had not taken you, somebody else would have had that pleasure. That's always the way it goes with girls like you!'

'Very well!' she said with deliberation. 'In obedience to the cowardly conventions of your society, you betray me and abandon me . . . You disown me . . . and believe me I'm not the sort of woman to put up with that kind of insult.'

'If you make a scandal', began the Baron coldly, 'I shall find myself obliged to close my doors to you.'

This was altogether too much for the poor creature's reckless and undauntable nature.

'To hell with your money and all your wealth!' she screamed, quite beside herself with rage. 'Get out of this house at once!'

'Think carefully what you're doing', murmured the Baron.

'Get out! Out of my sight!' she ordered, her lips trembling; then—and such a thing had never happened to him before—she pushed him outside, her fist clenched and menacing, as if she were about to strike him.

At that, Baron Steinfeld went away and vanished.

Chapter III

THE FIRST STEP

Early one morning, some four months later, a lady of elegant appearance who seemed to be waiting for someone, was pacing up and down before the house in Kärntner-strasse where the Baron lived.

As Baron Steinfeld came out of his residence, this lady, who was discreetly veiled, approached him rapidly and said:

'Do you recognise me?'

'Please do not make a scene in the street!' said the Baron curtly.

'Now that you have me turned away by your servants, I have no option but to oblige you to listen in the open street to the distasteful things which it pains me to have to tell you!'

'This is hardly a place for an interview.'

'Then come with me to my place', she said.

These two human beings who had formerly been so passionately in love now walked side by side in frigid silence. Still without saying a word they both mounted the staircase that led to the abode which not so long ago had been to them a paradise . . .

The Baron looked around him in surprise, for he scarcely recognised this appartment, which he had known so well before and where Anna Klauer still lived, but which he had now stayed away from for the greater part of a year.

The pictures and the expensive mirrors had disappeared from the walls, the rooms had been stripped of part of their luxurious furnishings. The abandoned mistress had sold them in order not to have to sell herself or not to have to beg; for, after having lived the life of a princess for three years, work now seemed to her degrading.

Going into her bedroom, she nonchalantly beckoned to the Baron to follow her, and then seating herself upon the Turkish divan the luxury of which was reminiscent of past splendours, she invited him to sit down too. Then she threw off the costly shawl that enveloped her shoulders. She cast a piercing glance at the Baron, which caused him to change colour: he grew pale.

Lowering her eyes, she went on: 'I am afraid that I am about to become a mother. In any other circumstances, I should not have made any attempt to see you again, but now I have certain duties to fulfil towards my child and myself, and you too have duties to us both; and so I cannot think of allowing you to abandon me in this condition, or leaving either the child or myself in distress!'

Her eyes brimmed with tears.

'Calm yourself', said the Baron, seizing her hand. 'I have always taken care of you, so long as you didn't have me thrown out; and today I feel more than ever impelled to come to your assistance. I will find you a nice house somewhere on the outskirts of town, settle an income on you and pay off the arrears of your allowance.'

'Is that all?' asked Anna coldly. 'Have you no conception of what you owe me? It's not your gold, it's *you* I want ... '

'Me? I don't follow you . . .'

'It's your duty to marry me.'

'What are you thinking of?' exclaimed the Baron, flying into a rage. 'What would my family say if I married the daughter of working-class parents?'

'You saw nothing wrong in seducing the daughter of working-class parents, in making her your mistress; and your family had no fault to find when you kissed the feet of a working-class girl and let her trample on you', exclaimed Anna in reply.

'You are inhuman', remarked the Baron.

'I beg you', said Anna in tears, 'save my honour, save our child. You can still behave like an honest man and I would be to you a faithful wife, obedient and affectionate, which is more than all the princesses and countesses will ever be. Don't abandon me; don't make me unhappy;

don't condemn me to a life of vice ... I am proud, I will not let myself be betrayed, I will not tolerate it! ...'

'I do not fear your vengeance', said the Baron. Thereupon he stood up, and, picking up his hat with a disdainful smile, he added: 'I will keep my promise to provide for you, in spite of your foolish threats. You know my address. If you should have need of me, write to me ...'

'Is that your last word?'

'Yes.'

'Very well then, get out of here! I would rather starve to death or steal and die than ever in future be beholden to you for anything at all, even if it were only a simple mouthful of bread', she exclaimed. Her voice was vibrant with emotion. 'Nevertheless, remember this moment; as for me, I shall never forget it.'

They turned their backs on each other and Baron Steinfeld went away slowly but without any feeling of shame or remorse towards the unfortunate girl whom he was thus betraying. Come what might, there was no turning back now.

Some days later he took Countess Thurn to the altar, and when the ceremony was over went to Paris to spend his honeymoon in the company of his young bride. On the same day of her interview with her faithless lover, Anna Klauer sold the rest of her furniture and all of her jewels. However she retained her expensive clothes, not without deliberate intent. The proceeds of all these sales brought in the considerable sum of 60,000 guilders. Thus, for the time being, she found herself safe from want.

Then she set herself up in a small residence on the outskirts of Laxenburg and shut herself in there to await the return of the Baron to Vienna; but this time events proved too strong for her. She could not carry her plan into execution and everything turned out differently from what she wanted and from what she had foreseen.

One of her old servants, who was still in her employ, had undertaken to keep an eye on the comings and goings of Baron Steinfeld. Now on the very day that she felt the first labour pains, this servant came to bring her the fatal news that, provisionally, the traitor would not be returning to Vienna, but would be spending the rest of the summer in a castle in the south of Bohemia belonging to his wife.

This news came at a bad time. At the decisive moment, the wretched girl did herself violence and thus took the first terrible step on the road to crime, without precisely being aware of the frightful consequences that her act might have.

As the afternoon wore on, her poor proud heart had but one thought: to hide her shame from the world. Until then, she had managed to conceal from everyone her true condition. But from now on, she might at any moment betray herself. She made up her mind rapidly therefore, wrapped herself in a shawl, and took herself to the Laxenburg Park, where she hid in the darkness.

Night came. It was a black, starless night. Silent, heartbroken, completely desperate, breathing no sound of complaint, Anna Klauer lay down under a dark pine bush uttering no cry that might reveal her presence. The strength of character of this unfortunate girl was such that in the midst of the most frightful sufferings she did not let a single sigh escape her, or shed a single tear.

When at last, she held her newborn child in her arms, she stifled its first cries by means of a handkerchief, but, in violation of all maternal sentiment, she was not filled with joy at the sight of the poor innocent; then, summoning all her remaining strength, she dragged herself painfully with savage energy to the edge of a pond nearby and almost unconsciously let the poor baby slip into the water.

Then she broke down and wept bitterly.

One hour later, she returned home. Nobody who saw her would have suspected from her appearance or her bearing that she had been doing anything but taking her usual stroll.

The following day she packed all her belongings and went back to Vienna, and, leaving the city the same evening, made her way to Budweis, with the purpose of seeking the Baron on his estates at the Austrian-Bavarian frontier; she was going—impelled by some mystic force, some hidden power—she knew not where.

Chance came to her aid. At the little inn in Budweis, where she had descended from the coach, there happened to be a Hungarian woman, a pedlar, who was at the point of death. A little girl and a boy of tender years were weeping and mourning at their poor mother's bedside. The woman accepted Anna Klauer's good offices and Anna stayed with her until she had breathed her last.

Then she closed the woman's eyes, and took possession of her papers, even of her passport, which she—as if it had been her own document—took to the Burgomaster to be visa'd. Finally she took the trouble to see that the poor orphans were looked after, and handed over to the Mayor on their behalf the handsome sum of one thousand guilders.

Then she made her way to the Baron's castle, leaving her bags behind her in the name of Sarolta Kuliseki— the name of the unfortunate pedlar-woman from Munich. She quickly hired a coach to take her to Goldrain, the site of the very castle at which Steinfeld and his young bride were staying. Barely a hundred yards from this castle there stood a village.

She got out of the carriage before the inn, paid the coachman and dismissed him. Then, in the dining-room, she had a coffee, and asked the hotelier some questions which for the time being would completely mislead him as to the plans that she had devised against the Baron and make it seem that she was planning a simple afternoon stroll. As a matter of fact, she set out across the fields in the opposite direction to the castle, but when she reached the high road, she retraced her steps and made her way towards it.

Darkness was falling as she approached the castle, so that without difficulty and without being seen she was able to reach a large terrace which, from the dining-room, gave on to gardens filled with clusters of orange- and lemon-trees, by which it was surrounded.

Lightly and nimbly, Anna climbed the steps of this terrace, from which, hidden among the foliage of an orange-tree, she was able to see all that was going on in the room.

Her breast heaved with heavy sighs as she watched the man, whom she had formerly loved and now only detested, beside his young wife, who was marvellously and beautifully dressed and gleaming with jewels. They were taking tea together and he was kissing her and toying with her as he served her, and she was receiving his attentions with tender smiles.

Then, the demon of hate that slept in Anna's heart suddenly awoke: she drew from her pocket two pistols of which the Baron had some time previously made her a present, and loaded them.

At the very moment when the Baroness was offering her purple lips to her bridegroom's kisses, Anna, aiming through the open window, quickly fired first at the woman, and then at her ex-lover; she saw Baron Steinfeld slump heavily to the floor, and then, springing like a tigress, she made off across the park and soon reached the border of the adjoining woods.

When she came to some high ground, she listened carefully, and, as everything was quiet, she reloaded her pistols. She was ready for anything . . .

After having rested for a few moments, she went on her way, absorbed by two all-pervading thoughts. The first was: I have killed him; I am avenged! The second: I must get away and begin a new life, a life whose only rules shall be to hate men and to care for no-one but myself!

Chapter IV

IF YOU WANT TO COMMAND YOU MUST LEARN TO OBEY

Over mountainous paths, previously traversed by audacious smugglers, Anna Klauer made her way until she reached the small Bavarian town of Gravenau. From there, she got a peasant to take her in his cart to the nearest railway station. Some hours later, she found herself in Munich.

In that royal city, she at last regained full self-possession, and set about examining the pedlar-woman's passport minutely. The age and the different indications it bore by way of personal description might equally well apply to Anna herself, except for one thing which she noted with a shock: red hair!

Her shock, however, did not last long: after a brief moment's reflection, she had triumphantly solved this difficulty. In the Viennese newspapers she had read about the wife of a famous painter, herself an artiste in a suburban theatre, who had changed from a brunette to a golden blonde using a method discovered in Paris.

Consequently, she need have no fear that the forgery would be discovered, and she could use Sarolta Kuliseki's passport and pass herself off as the dead woman.

She first went to see a hairdresser who had been pointed out to her as the leading coiffeur in Munich and asked him if he were conversant with the Parisian discovery. As this man assured her he was, she told him with a laugh that she would much prefer to have absolutely mahogany-red hair rather than hair that was golden blonde.

The hairdresser having undertaken to dye Anna's hair to the tint desired, within the space of a few days, she left him feeling completely reassured, sent her suitcase to the station and went to book up at a modest hotel.

While the hairdresser's treatment lasted, she did not leave her room and had all her meals served to her there. But when, about the fifteenth day, her brown hair had become a ruddy gold like that of the Nibelungen, making a strange contrast with her dark eyes and giving to her whole countenance a certain something that was devilishly enchanting, she covered her face with a thick veil, left her hotel and took a room elsewhere by the month.

There she changed her clothes—those she had worn in Budweis and in Goldrain—and, one hour later, ravishingly beautiful and certainly seeming to resemble in all respects the Goddess of Love rising from the waves, dressed in white cambric trimmed with lace, she could be seen strolling with a light and springy step along the streets of Munich.

She stopped in front of the displays in the most luxurious shop windows, contemplating all those beautiful things with the air of a woman who had had her share of them, who still possessed them, and could, if she desired, possess still more of them at any time she chose.

As she found herself being admired by all the elegant men who came and went, there began to form in her mind a serious resolution, while a playful smile hovered at her lips.

She broke completely with her past and she swore to herself to pursue thenceforward, without regard for others, without weakening, without pity, the relentless way that she had chosen, that she had traced out for herself, and follow through to that definite goal to which her hatred of men and her infernal selfishness led her.

She wanted to become a great lady, rich and powerful, to enable herself to take revenge on the whole human race for the treachery of one man who had left her no other sentiment than scorn.

Nevertheless, she was not yet within sight of her goal, and so she almost resolved to go on the stage, either as a dancer or an actress.

She had often heard that women of the theatre, despite their inferior origins, and their frivolous conduct, finally managed to become the legitimate wives of barons, counts or princes, and sometimes even regents married them morganatically.

A single unforeseen circumstance occurred to cause her to make up her mind. On a wall at a street corner was displayed a poster. It said: CIBALDI CIRCUS—GRAND SHOW TODAY, etc., etc. She returned home and reserved a box. The show was just beginning when she made her appearance at the circus.

All eyes turned immediately to the new and unusual though dazzling apparition, and Anna Klauer, or rather, as she called herself from now on, Sarolta Kuliseki, proved so amiable as she flirted with each in turn, that at the end of the show a dozen slaves from all classes of society had chained themselves to her triumphal chariot.

One of them, a young and elegant cavalry officer, was resourceful enough to wait for her at the exit, to follow her, and there and then offer her his arm and his company.

She looked him up and down, then burst out laughing. 'What do you take me for?' she said. 'I am not a young girl; girls have a heart, but I have no heart any more!' And thereupon she detached herself from the cavalry officer's arm and left him standing there utterly stupefied.

That same night, Sarolta made up her mind to become a circus bare-back rider. A beautiful bare-back rider was not, as she was well aware, anything new, but a beautiful bare-back rider who was at the same time virtuous could not fail to produce a certain kind of sensation among men of all classes, and she could enchain them and make them her slaves to her heart's content.

As for her, it was nothing but a game to pose as virtuous in the most heartless acceptation of the word, for she was no longer capable of loving, and she could enrich herself in this way. The world was opening up before her, and, in her struggle with it, she was bound to emerge victorious.

The brilliant lighting of the circus and the elegant and aristocratic audience, the boldness of the art of *haute école*, even the rich, seductive costume of the horsewomen had completely fascinated her.

Early the next morning, wearing a costume of heavy dark velvet and, on her head, a little Mary Stuart bonnet of the same material trimmed with a flowing white feather, she went to see the *haute école* director, a professional riding-master, who, dazzled by her appearance, found little difficulty in admitting her to his troupe.

'You must not fall off even once, Madame', the agile little Italian with the bronze skin assured her nevertheless. 'If you want to command you must learn to obey. The training in our art is hard and stern, and we could not, for our part, run the risk of undertaking your instruction if there was a chance that you might leave us as soon as you had no longer the patience to try out some new and difficult task.

'You must therefore sign a paper according to the terms of which you will engage yourself to stay with us for three years. Your work will be a real form of slavery, but it cannot be otherwise: our discipline is an iron one, quite military! . . . '

Sarolta showed not a moment's hesitation: she knew that her steely nature, her satanic will, were capable of overcoming all obstacles. So she signed there and then and without saying a word, the terrible contract, although, a little later, dressed as she was in rough working clothes that she had had to put on for a private lesson, the beauties of the circus had robbed her of a good many of her illusions.

The very next day she went to see the circus owner, Cibaldi, °and informed him that she was ready to place herself in his care, to join the Munich troupe, and thereafter to go with them on a tour of the North.

She began her classes in Cologne. Events were soon to prove that she not only had to contend with the difficulties of *haute école* and the bad temper of the riding-master, who, with the aid of a whip and the mysterious power of his curses and Italian insults, seemed to think that he could train people as he trained horses, but also to endure the chaffing of her male colleagues and the jealousy of her female ones, and particularly of the directress, Arabella Cibaldi, a gaunt little Italian woman with a splenetic temperament.

The husband of the latter, a veritable demon and sort of executioner's assistant at the riding-school, was no less a perfect lamb where the seductive Sarolta was concerned and directed all his attentions to this Sarolta—for so Anna Klauer called herself in her profession of bare-back rider—so much so that the skinny Arabella became greatly put out by this.

Thus Sarolta learned to leapfrog over her difficulties as

though she were playing a game. From the very first day, she gave evidence of the skill and daring on horseback of a consummate Amazon. She undertook the most dangerous exercises with a kind of mocking courage that savoured of experience, and invariably displayed an ironbound discipline which was absolutely indefatigable. She obeyed the riding-master's orders with the same blind passivity as a horse would have done.

However, the more satisfaction she gave Cibaldi, the more she had to put up with from the others.

Monsieur Jacques, the clown, had taken to amusing the whole troupe at her expense, taking the liberty of making the silliest jokes about her, but, instead of bursting into tears or bemoaning her cruel fate—as any other novice might have done in her place—she only laughed at it all, and her good humour proved disarming to the joker.

The vulgarity of Brown, the strong man bare-back rider, met with nothing but the most refined politeness on her part. To the pinpricks and calumnies of Miss Stanette, the leading female equestrian performer, she replied with obliging humility, with countless little services and complaisances; and as for the mischievous tricks of that young rascal Williams, she soon put a stop to them by means of gifts, of titbits and of attentions that were almost motherly. Finally, whenever Signora Arabella ventured to come to the riding-school and to prompt her with a stroke of the whip, Sarolta invariably kissed her hand after the lesson, saying with platitudinous assurance that she considered herself fortunate to be struck by her, for 'The hand that loves well does well to chastise!'

Thus she managed, little by little, to win over everyone, to make herself indispensable to everyone, and, without being aware of it herself, to make the most of everyone.

From the circus director and his wife she learned good Italian, from Monsieur Jacques the most elegant French; Mr Brown, who in reality was a Hungarian named Matschlausie, taught her Magyar, his own language, which she soon succeeded in speaking like a real Hungarian woman. As for Miss Stanette, whose name was actually Wilhelmine Sporner, a native of Hanover, she helped her to exchange the soft Viennese dialect for the harsh but correct High German.

When at last, at Frankfurt-am-Main, she appeared for the first time in public and carried off a dazzlingly successful performance, she—hitherto so mistreated and made fun of—became the spoilt child of the director and of the whole troupe; it was now her turn to play the tyrant of those who had tyrannised over her.

No matter where the troupe gave shows, Sarolta was pursued by the assiduities of the most handsome and wealthiest men in all the places she went to; but she affected such an incredible frigidity towards their advances that she soon acquired the universal nickname of "The Virtuous Equestrienne".

Chapter V

THE VIRTUOUS EQUESTRIENNE

The three-year contract which Sarolta had signed with the circus director had all but run its full term, when the troupe was performing in Budapest and causing such a sensation there, particularly owing to the beauty and intrepidity of Sarolta, that a great part of the country's nobility forgathered in the Hungarian capital in order to attend the shows given by the Cibaldi Circus, since for every true Magyar there is nothing to surpass this spectacle.

Now it was not at all within Signor Cibaldi's scheme of things to lose at such a time the very pearl of his troupe; and so he applied himself to the business of persuading Sarolta to sign a new contract. To accomplish this, he literally cringed before her and overwhelmed her with the most flattering epithets, the most affectionate diminutives and the most enthusiastic superlatives.

Nobody would have presumed to open the barrier for her or to help her to dismount from her horse, for it had to be one of her gallants who invariably, on such occasions, hastened to her assistance, though she, without the least acknowledgement, without even casting a friendly glance in his direction, would place her foot in the proffered hand and spring lightly to the ground.

Now she was mistress of the situation and was very well capable of playing the consummate despot, just as before she had behaved like an obedient daughter and pupil. She had her own wardrobe now, and woe betide any lady of the troupe who happened to be in her path when she appeared, or who, being ordered to get out of the way failed to obey the injunction promptly: she was forthwith pressed into service as a lady's maid.

She no longer spared even the directress herself, who now would pull off or put on her boots with enthusiasm, though she generally received only a slap by way of acknowledgment. They were all her slaves and she reigned over them, with the aid of a riding-whip which she applied with as little discrimination to that athletic figure Brown as to the puny little clown Monsieur Jacques.

And it was by no means necessarily a leg-pull or some act of disobedience that called forth the application of her flexible sceptre; she ill-treated people for pleasure, she tormented those about her on purpose, and if anyone rebelled against her, she would pass sentence on him and chastise him there and then like a refractory Negro slave.

Whoever was in her presence trembled before her, and the more she made herself feared, the more it delighted her, the more it seemed to make her feel happy.

Even in Pest, great lords and financiers, young and old, could not approach her except by successfully negotiating some intricate intrigue. Sarolta carried austerity to such a point that she not only returned their romantic notes, but also their bouquets of flowers, and, especially, their gifts.

Besides, other members of society did not fail to point out to all those admirers who so futilely sought the good graces of this strange beauty her haughty and imperious character, so that, among the whole of the elegant society of Pest, Sarolta was soon regarded as the most austerely virtuous of women and a woman of utterly diabolical cruelty.

As a result, the extraordinary reputation that she had acquired excited every man who yearned at the side of a good and faithful wife to be ill-treated by a heartless courtesan, and each day brought new triumphs to the virtuous equestrienne.

One morning, while Sarolta was resting after one of her most tiring performances and was still propped up on silken cushions, her maid came to announce that a gentleman desired to speak with her at once.

She instructed the maid to tell him to come back later, but he would not be dismissed in this way and solicited with even more insistence the favour of an audience, handing in his card in support of his request.

Sarolta, with an impatient gesture, took the card from the silver tray that the chambermaid held out to her, and read: 'Julius, Prince Parkany'. She rested her beautiful head on her superbly moulded arm, and seemed to be deep in thought; then she said at last: 'Let him come in.'

The Prince advanced briskly right up to her couch; and as the redoubtable woman swept back the dishevelled hair that framed her face like the rays of the sun, he could perceive amid the seductively soft folds of the dark fur covering, which she had thrown back on to her shoulders, her breasts as of a marble Venus, more revealed than veiled.

He stood there for a moment as if petrified at the sight, then, recovering from his abstraction, he fell on his knees before her.

Sarolta surveyed him with a sly and penetrating expression, but she did not send him away: she took pleasure in the sight of him. It did not enter her mind, however, that she might one day love him.

Nevertheless this handsome and fabulously wealthy magnate, aged about fifty, did seem to her precisely the very man she had been waiting for, whom, for three years, she had incessantly been seeking, in order to put into execution the daring and highly ambitious plan she had been harbouring.

'My dear lady', said the Prince, 'do not take it amiss if I come straight to the point. I know of your virtue, as I am aware also of your despotic character; I realise that you tolerate only slaves.

'I will not say anything to you of love, but I will permit myself to tell you that, ever since I saw you in your riding act yesterday evening for the first time, I have worshipped you, as I never have worshipped any woman before; that everything I possess is at your disposal, and that I desire nothing but the right to be your slave.'

'Oh, come now! You must want something more than that!' Sarolta replied with a playful smile. 'I should be lying if I were to say to you: "I love you". It may well be that I am quite incapable of loving any man. Be that as it may, you do awaken an extraordinary interest in me. Perhaps I may today put to you the same question that you yourself yesterday, from your own box, put to me, and to which never, in the course of my entire career, have I permitted myself to answer in a positive way to anybody, whoever it might be.'

'You make me inexplicably happy!' exclaimed the Prince. 'Then you will have the graciousness to permit me to serve you as if you were my mistress and I your humble servant?'

'I am not accustomed to pretend and I am sometimes inconsiderate in my frankness', was Sarolta's reply,— 'because I am too proud to conceal my sentiments or to hide my thoughts. For that reason I must ask you to listen to what I expect from you:

'If the thrill that the professional equestrienne inspires in you evaporates, then you must leave me and forget

142

me. Not only will I not bear you any malice for so doing, but I will be grateful to you for it. If, on the other hand, your feelings concerning that woman are such as you say they are and you are furthermore convinced that that woman retains the hold that attracts you to her only through the dread that your enthusiasm may prove to be a blazing straw and that, if she were to give herself to you, she would lose all the dazzling advantages that she derives from her profession, then I will be yours.'

'Can you be serious in what you are saying, Sarolta?' exclaimed the Prince exultantly.

'I have never been more serious.'

'Then, you belong to me.'

'Not yet; you must first hear my conditions', replied the equestrienne. 'In a fortnight's time my engagement with Cibaldi comes to an end; on the day that my contract expires I will belong to you, but only providing that I can turn my back on the riding-school for ever. Guarantee me an independent existence—I care nothing for splendour or luxury—and, assuredly, unless it should happen that you don't love me any more, I will be yours!'

'Within one hour', he said 'everything will be arranged. Until then, be good, my little despot!'

Thereupon he bowed very low and withdrew. Sarolta followed him with her eyes, and when he was gone she gave vent to a ringing peal of laughter. It was the laughter of a demon triumphant . . .

Chapter VI

Ecclesiastical Co-operation

Dominating everyone like a queen, Sarolta, the beautiful equestrienne, formerly Anna Klauer, now resided in the ancient castle of the Parkany family, as the mistress of the Prince.

There she lived in fabulously luxurious style, and

amused herself by ill-treating with the most refined cruelty both the man who adored her and all his *entourage*.

Indeed, the Prince seemed, in the eyes of the world, merely to fulfil, like an indulgent lover, Sarolta's every whim, but, in reality, he was madly infatuated by her and loved her with irrational frenzy: one look from her, one gesture of her hand, one smile on her lips, impelled him to support any sacrifice, any torment that it might please this woman to inflict upon him.

Just as previously in the circus, everyone at the castle, as well as in the villages within the Prince's jurisdiction, trembled before her.

She gave all the orders, and she herself inflicted, most of the time, all the punishments, assisted by an odious old woman by the name of Halka, and two buxom, strapping, good-looking girls, one named Iela, the other Ersabeth, whom she had chosen from the neighbourhood and taken into her service.

If any servant or peasant had done anything remiss as far as this female tyrant was concerned, he was ordered to report immediately to Sarolta in her bedchamber, where he generally found her reclining on a luxurious divan; she would remind him of his faults and announce the punishment that he had incurred.

No sooner did he hear the sentence than he was seized from behind by the two wenches, who, until then, had remained concealed behind a heavy curtain. The two women, before he had even had time to realise what was about to happen, had bound him securely hand and foot.

While all the time taunting the unfortunate victim with the cruellest jokes, Sarolta's two assistant executioners would open the trap door that led to the ground floor and drag the poor wretch down a winding staircase to a kind of dungeon situated at the bottom of the stairs, followed by the cruel tyrant herself.

There the condemned fellow would be tied to a stake, while Sarolta, assisted by Iela and Ersabeth, lashed him with a pair of long whips until the blood ran, deriving from this work a kind of diabolical pleasure.

Then they would leave him there all day long, his body faint with hunger and tugging at his aching limbs. To see men suffer had become for the former equestrienne a source of sensual delight.

The Prince's friends and neighbours who visited the Parkany castle and took part in the dazzling banquets, the hunts and sleigh-parties organised by Sarolta, constituted a kind of court for this imperious and petulant woman, although they had had, too, on more than one occasion, to endure her sovereign whims and capricious cruelties.

One day, she caused a veritable torrent to pour from the ceiling on the assembled company; on another occasion, she made all her guests at dinner sit upon stinging-nettles. She treated them all, with the exception of two, little better than her domestic staff. One of these favourites was a young and handsome nobleman whose estates were contiguous with those of the Prince.

His name was Emerich Bethlemy. From the exchange of the very first glances, this man had awakened strange sensations in the marble breast of this heartless woman, and more than once she chanced to give herself away where he was concerned, either through lack of self-control, or through some slip of the tongue,—which only seemed to baffle everyone.

But Bethlemy, who esteemed the Prince as much as the Prince's mistress hated him, adopted towards the imperious woman's advances an attitude of coldness which rendered any relations between them impossible and only served to enliven the flame of passion that the nobleman had inspired in Sarolta.

The second man who struck her as also worthy of her attention was Parkany's confessor, Father Pistian.

The latter, a young ecclesiastic of prepossessing appearance, whose chastity was overtaxed by celibacy, had conceived for Sarolta an infernal passion which he sought to excite still further by flirting with her, to such effect that, at last, she more or less took for granted his co-operation towards bringing her insidious plan to fruition.

One stifling summer evening, Father Pistian came to the castle and was conducted to Sarolta's bedchamber by the old hag Halka, the latter's confidante who, among the common people, was known under the name of "The old witch of Parkany". The Prince had gone to Pest, and Sarolta was expecting this visit from her beloved cleric and had prepared herself for it.

As he entered, she was seated in an armchair, wearing a flimsy négligé of Brussels lace openwork, and was reading a book. With a mere glance she dismissed the old woman. Father Pistian then took up a position beside Sarolta and seized her hand, pressing it against his lips which were burning with passion.

'You did well to come', said the cunning coquette; 'I feel so unhappy today, so sad, that you must console me.'

'How may that be possible, since I myself have such great need of comfort?' replied the priest.

'You?'

'You know, Sarolta, how much I adore you!'

'You must be joking, surely. How could you love the mistress whom everybody detests?'

'Ah, if you only knew how much I suffer', sighed Pistian, 'you would not be so unkind.'

'So you are unhappy, are you?' said Sarolta, 'and so am I. Let us consider together, then, whether there is not some way in which we can help each other. I do not deny that I could love you, but I could never, as the mistress of the Prince, run the risk of paying heed to your advances. If it were discovered, there would be nothing left for me but to beg for a living. You possess great influence over the Prince's soul; cause him to make me his wife and I will belong to you! . . . '

Pistian was transported with delight, and flung himself at the feet of the beautiful woman whom he adored and swore to serve her in everything, adding that, like a docile instrument, he would do whatever she demanded of him.

The Prince who, like all these aristocrats, often wilfully fell far short of observing the precepts of morality, was outwardly a pious devotee and regular churchgoer, never omitting to go regularly each month to confession. Father Pistian had until now been prudent enough not to remind him, except in a very indirect and almost vague way, of the need for all the faithful to observe the commandments of the Church.

But when, the next month, the Prince, with a humble and contrite spirit was kneeling in the penitent's pew, the priest began by haranguing him with grave remonstrances concerning his immorality vis-à-vis the Church and State in relation to his irregular union with Sarolta and, finally, demanded that he must give her up under pain of incurring all the punishments both temporal and of the hereafter.

The Prince shed tears and showed signs of the most profound repentance, but protested that it would cost him his life if he had to cut himself off now from this woman who had become his idol.

At last, the sly confessor pronounced the counsel that he had purposely so cleverly withheld. He advised the Prince to marry Sarolta. The poor sinner breathed again and extolled this precept, saying that without delay he would conform to it.

Back in the castle, he asked for Sarolta. She had gone to confession, replied the old woman. One hour later, the beautiful girl dressed in a sombre gown, her eyes reddened by weeping, herself returned and, kneeling on her praying-stool, she gave the appearance of being profoundly absorbed in her devotions. The Prince came in but hovered at the threshold of the room, lacking the courage to interupt Sarolta.

She had heard his steps, but pretended to have noticed nothing. Then at last she got up, uttered a long sigh, and sponged away her tears. Turning towards the Prince, she seemed startled to see him there, supported herself momentarily with the back of the chair, and then, seeming to cast aside all vestige of pride, she flung herself on her knees before him.

'We must separate', she exclaimed, feigning violent

sobs that convulsed her. 'I beseech you, do not make this separation more difficult for me than it is already. Have pity on me; let me go.'

'No, no! Never...' murmured the nobleman, as he raised his beautiful beloved to her feet and gently rested her head against his breast. 'We will never separate, Sarolta. I have for long experienced the same remorse that today seems to be tormenting you, and I have now resolved to put an end to this situation which is unworthy of both of us. I want our union to be consecrated by the Church.'

'Thank you, oh thank you a thousand times! ...' exclaimed Sarolta. 'But how can I have deserved such a sacrifice?'

'By showing me what a good and faithful wife you can be', said the Prince.

'Yes, and that I will be until the end of my days', murmured Sarolta. 'Yes, I will be your servant, and I will obey you like a slave ...'

With the haste of a love-sick swain incapable of restraining himself, the Prince took care to let his mother and his aunts know of his impending marriage to his beloved, which would be on All Saints Day. He personally supervised all the preparations.

At the express desire of Sarolta, whose every wish was an order for the Prince—the ceremony took place secretly in the castle chapel. The Prince himself led Sarolta to the altar.

Instead of a circlet of orange blossom, the former equestrienne wore a tiara glittering with diamonds; instead of the white gown of innocence, she had put on a dress of red velvet adorned with ermine, with a veil and train of white antique moire, relieved with Brussels lace. The witnesses were Emerich von Bethlemy and a certain old Count Czapari. After a sonorous homily on the sanctity of marriage, Father Pistian consecrated the newly-weds.

When Sarolta left the chapel on the arm of her husband, Prince Parkany, a strange smile hovered at the sensual lips of the new Princess. She had arrived at her goal at last . . .

The day after the ceremony, the Prince had to go to Pest again to do some shopping for his wife. Towards evening, Father Pistian was announced. When he came in, Sarolta, dressed in a diaphanous négligé, over which she had thrown a velvet jacket well trimmed with ermine, was reclining on a sumptuous divan. She greeted the priest with a laugh.

'You're in quite a hurry', she said, 'to come and collect your reward'.

'Could I love you so much if I were not?' replied Pistian.

'But do you realise what it means to be my slave?' replied the cruel beauty in a mocking tone. 'He who courts danger will succumb to it.'

'Then let me succumb', declared Pistian, beside himself.

He flung himself down beside her, while she, her face wreathed in smiles, enfolded him in her delightful arms! . . .

Chapter VII

THE WITCH OF PARKANY

From the day when Sarolta first put on the ermine of a princess she seemed to have changed completely. Her hatred of men, her need for mockery, seemed to have diminished, as also had her penchant for cruelty, which had caused her until then to be feared for ten leagues around.

Day by day the Prince was more and more surprised by the sweetness and affability which his wife now evinced, by the suppleness and kindliness of her every mood, and above all by the alacrity she showed thenceforward in anticipating his slightest wish and in acceding to it as soon as possible.

At every turn he thanked the priest for the counsel he had given him, every time causing the holy man the most profound embarrassment, for, as soon as he found himself alone with the Princess, he became the most impassioned lover.

Almost a year went by in this way, and, during all that time, the royal couple behaved like two love-birds. All Parkany's friends showed themselves smitten with his wife; the great ladies of the neighbourhood began to visit her, and even Emerich von Bethlemy himself began to take a fancy to her and secretly to convey to this woman his apologies for having too precipitately misjudged her.

One gloomy October evening, when a hurricane was rattling the windows of the old castle and howling down the chimneys, the Prince had gone to visit a neighbour's residence where a political meeting was taking place of people belonging to the same party. Sarolta was alone. Overcome by a sense of unspeakable melancholy and tedium, she wandered all over the vast building; at last she came to the servants' quarters situated on the ground floor, and there she asked after Halka, the witch of Parkany, as the common people called her.

Nobody ventured to supply any information about the old woman; but at last, after two further enquiries, the Princess again demanded to know where the witch was, and an insolent youngster named Ferenz, the Prince's valet, exclaimed: 'The old witch has gone up the tower to practise her magic spells!'

Thereupon, Sarolta began to ascend the steep steps of the narrow winding staircase that led to the tower, inhabited only by owls, ravens and rats.

As she reached the worm-eaten door of the tiny room situated immediately below the battlements and where, in the age of chivalry, the watchman sheltered, her ear was struck by the sounds of a strange droning song chanted by another female voice, and at that moment she was seized with fright. But Sarolta was not going to be intimidated by another woman, whoever she might be. She knocked loudly on the door and cried: 'Open, Halka, it's me. I have come to visit you in your witch's den.'

The door opened at once and the sinister old woman, swathed in a coarse black cloak, a red rag bound round her head like a turban, her face rugged and withered, welcomed her unexpected visitor with a friendly leer.

Sarolta saw with astonishment that she had entered a small arched room. On one of the walls there was fixed a kind of grate over the lighted fire of which stood all sorts of crucibles, retorts and matrasses; opposite stood an ancient cupboard blackened by time and full of glass phials and boxes of all colours.

In the corner, an assortment of plants and roots; in another a tall leather armchair, on the gilded top of which was perched a raven which was pecking and foraging about. Beside the armchair, there was a table similarly covered with crucibles, flasks and other utensils used by the old hag.

In the middle of this table glowed the warm light of a small red lamp whose crude illumination gave to the floor on which it fell the appearance of being stained with blood. Two great black cats, who kept the old woman company, were warming their paws by the fire.

'Pray sit down, gracious Princess', said Halka, leading Sarolta towards the armchair.

The raven flapped its wings, croaked and alighted on the floor.

The beautiful woman took on a strange expression as she sat there, in her majestic jacket of red velvet trimmed with ermine, amid the fantastic spectres of that dusty dwelling.

'Now', said Sarolta with a laugh, 'let me see some examples of your art; initiate me a little into your secrets.'

'Why not?' replied the old woman. 'I know very well that you will not betray me.'

'Who told you that?'

'The stars', said the old woman in a low voice.

'And is that all you have to say about me?'

'No.'

'Then speak.'

'I knew that you would come to me, Madame and amiable Princess, and that poor old Halka would be able to be of use to you.'

'In what respect and in what way do you think you can be useful to me?' asked Sarolta briskly and almost abashed.

'Through the help of him who knows all nature and its mysterious forces and to whom several of them serve as precepts', murmured the old woman.

Thereupon, she went to her cupboard and took out two dark phials.

'Here', said she, indicating the latter, 'are the means of recovering youth and beauty, but thank God you have no need for them at present.'

'But who knows? . . . perhaps in time!'

'Then you will tell me so, and I will surely and willingly help you', whispered the old woman. 'But alas! there will never be such an easy opportunity to make use of the best of my knowledge.'

'Is that so?' asked Sarolta.

The old woman got down from her stool and flung herself at the feet of the Princess, and said: 'Have you never heard of a certain Hungarian lady, whose name escapes me, who was anxious to preserve eternal youth? That was more than two hundred years ago.'

'You mean the Countess Bathory.'

'The very one. Well, do you know what method she used?'

'No, I don't.'

'The most infallible,—she bathed in human blood.'

'Really . . . That's frightful.'

'What is so shocking about that?' continued the old woman. 'In former times people had slaves who were just right for that task, and—even today—what woman does not know men whom she hates and who are enemies she would sacrifice with pleasure in order to prolong her own life and youth. However, we will return to this subject some other time, for I see that you have not come to me to be initiated into this method of preserving beauty, but for something quite different.'

'You think so?'

The old woman handed Sarolta a little flask of a dark colour.

'What is this?'

'Poison!'

Sarolta seized the bottle eagerly. After a moment's hesitation, she murmured: 'If you are willing to serve me faithfully, Halka, I will reward you as only a queen can. Before everyone you must hold your tongue.'

'That advice is unnecessary', said the old woman with a sinister cackle. 'Fate has so far treated me badly enough to convince me that it brings nothing but suffering. I am hardly likely to betray you, since, even if it is you who fail to keep your word, we shall both go down into the abyss together! . . . '

Sarolta was startled.

'Once again', said the old woman, 'I assure you, you can do nothing without me. I know your plan, I have read it in the stars. You wish to be free; to obey is not in your nature; in your breast lurks a need for absolute domination. Your plan will succeed; everything will turn out favourably for you in all respects, and what is more you will have the sweet enjoyment of satiating your revenge on an enemy to the full; nevertheless, whatever happens, do nothing without first consulting the old witch.'

'I will send for you when I have need of you', said the Princess.

'Until then, may God protect Your Grace.'

From the next morning onwards, Sarolta shut herself up with the old woman and discussed with her the plan which since the day before they had already begun to concoct between them.

Halka advised her above all to choose a person whom she could with all safety accuse of having committed the crime.

Sarolta cast her eyes upon Ferenz, the Prince's valet, and immediately conceived a plot as bold as it was exceedingly clever.

She would burst with haste into her husband's study and demand that he punish his valet, whom she would accuse of having made an attack upon her honour . . .

The Prince attached the greatest credence to what his wife affirmed. Red with anger, he paid no attention to the denials of the unfortunate Ferenz, but had him seized by his henchmen, bound to a whipping-bench and beaten with canes until he lost consciousness.

When he came to himself, he received the order to leave the castle at once. He was, however, still unable to move, so that the henchmen left him lying in his quarters.

When night came, Sarolta, pretending to be indisposed, went to lie down in her bedchamber, where the old woman was already awaiting her. It was the Prince's custom to read until eleven o'clock, the hour at which Ferenz usually brought him the nightcap that he took before going to bed. This time it was Sarolta herself who appeared unexpectedly before the Prince.

'It is through me', she said with the sweetest of smiles, 'that Ferenz is unable today to perform his usual service, so I have come in his place.'

She handed the Prince a golden goblet, from which he was accustomed to drink, but beforehand she pretended to moisten her own lips and to taste it.

'Your health!' exclaimed the Prince as he raised the goblet to his lips. Suddenly the cup fell from his hands and rolled over the floor. The Prince tried to raise himself, but at the same moment fell back upon the pillow.

Sarolta then approached the bed with the calm, cold air of a doctor and placed her hand on her husband's heart.

He was dead! . . .

Presently the old woman came in, took the little phial containing the remainder of the poison, and made as if to leave the room.

'What are you going to do?' asked the Princess.

'I am going to put it into the pocket of Ferenz's livery', mumbled the witch.

'He is sleeping in the servants' quarters', said the Princess. 'Take care that no one sees you.'

'Oh, tonight they are already asleep!' said Halka, laughing. 'I mixed something harmless with their bedtime drinks, so that we are perfectly safe.'

So saying, she went away, while Sarolta retired to her room, undressed and went to sleep as tranquilly as though she had just committed a good action.

The next morning, she woke up all the castle by ringing the bell with all her might. The Prince was found dead in his bed, there was still poison in the goblet which had been served to him and some of the same poison in a small phial on the unfortunate Ferenz. The latter was immediately clapped in irons and brought before the judge.

The Princess took part in the proceedings in the capacity of a witness. She maintained emphatically that only Ferenz could be the culprit. On the day when the murder was committed, he had tried to violate her and the Prince had had him severely whipped, and it was clear that, to get his revenge, he had poisoned her poor husband, and if that were not proof enough some of this same poison which had so suddenly caused the death of the Prince had been found upon him.

Ferenz was condemned to death. All the way to the gallows he protested his innocence in vain. He was handed over to the executioner.

From her carriage, reclining nonchalantly upon white cushions, her lorgnette well focused on her wretched victim, the Princess seemed to feast her eyes upon the frightful convulsions of his death throes.

The Prince's will constituted her sole legatee of the Parkany castle, of all his other goods, as well as his colossal fortune.

Chapter VIII

THE HYENA OF THE PLAIN

The poisoner had been shrewd enough, after the Prince's death, to put on widow's weeds and observe the strictest mourning, feigning a grief that bordered on excess. It did not seem enough that she should abstain from everything that might be considered a pleasure of any kind: she banished such things from her residence and would allow no visitor to enter her chamber, or even enter the castle itself.

She went so far as to let rumour circulate that she slept in a coffin, her bedroom hung with black drapes, and that she spent the day in prayer and pious practices.

The truth is that the old witch, her two women confidantes, Ersabeth and Iela, and Father Pistian, were the only visitors admitted to her apartments. The priest would come under the pretext of bringing to the widow the consolations of religion, but in reality to gratify his sensual desires.

One day, Bethlemy also came to present his condolences to the Princess. He knew from experience that a visiting-card alone would not cause her door to be opened and that she most adroitly circumvented anyone who importuned her. However, it turned out on this occasion very differently.

He was admitted and found Sarolta wearing a very simple black dress, her head covered with a widow's veil. The sombre simplicity of that stern attire, unrelieved by any ornament, seemed to lend an even more dazzling attraction to her devilish beauty. She offered him her hand and then made signs to him to be seated.

After an exchange of the usual platitudes, Bethlemy rose to go.

'You wish to leave me so soon?' said the Princess poignantly. 'Have you really no presentiment of what you mean to me already, and of what I hope from you in the future? I am a poor shipwrecked soul, who glimpses land. All my hopes rest on you. Do not abandon me.'

'In what way can I be of service to you?' asked Bethlemy coldly.

'Don't be so formal', replied Sarolta, 'and please don't speak to me in that stand-offish tone. That will get us nowhere. I have to tell you everything—everything—but help me to break the ice, if you have the courage. I love you, Bethlemy, with all the strength of my energetic soul. My fate is in your hands. I offer you my hand. You can save me, you alone,—unless you refuse. Woe betide you and woe betide all men, if you persist in scorning me! So, what have you to say?'

'I am an honest man, Princess', replied the young nobleman. 'I do not scorn you, but I cannot love you.'

'You refuse my hand?' exclaimed Sarolta.

Bethlemy bowed very low and withdrew.

The forceful and hitherto so cruel woman crumpled to the floor and began to sob. For more than an hour, a violent struggle raged in her breast. She rose at last, resigned, cold as marble.

Thenceforward, she was resolved for all extremes: anything which could be called love, pity, circumspection, had been erased from her heart. From then on, her only rule of conduct would be the exercise of her revenge on the human race, the practice and the enjoyment of cruelty.

She made up her mind to carry out a plan as adventurous as it was reckless, which she had been nourishing secretly since the death of her husband, and which she now promised to carry through to its drastic conclusion with the full measure of her infernal lewdness, her bestial cruelty and her bloodthirsty instincts.

As night fell, the old witch of Parkany presented to the Princess a man who had been born on the empty plain, who knew no overlord: he was a *betyar*, a robber.

His name was Eyula Bartany. He was short of stature, but of Herculean build, and aged about forty.

Sarolta received him with undisguised curiosity, and, not without first having regaled him with a bottle of old *tokay,* she got him to relate to her some of the episodes of his life, including his crimes.

Once, thanks to the perfidy of a girl of loose morals with whom he was in love, Eyula was persuaded to leave his parents' tavern and to join up with a gang of bandits called *czegenyi legeniek.** By dint of courage and cunning he managed to make himself so conspicuous that very soon he became a chief of a band of fifteen men.

'You are my man', said the Princess, after having listened to the brigand's story. 'I see very well that you are no ordinary vagabond, but on the contrary one of those resolute men who stand up to the tyrants and take revenge on hypocrites, plying them with the deadly poison that infests our souls.

'I too have been betrayed, trampled underfoot, and my sole happiness would be to avenge myself on men, to torture them, to ill-treat them, and feast my eyes on their death agonies. I am rich and powerful. You are brave and you know all the shifts and tricks of your bloody profession. Nothing can frighten either you or me. We must, therefore, become allies and make a treaty, a contract.

'Listen to my proposition. Place your whole band in my service, and enlist, at my expense, other courageous and determined fellows,—no mere novices, mind! You will conform to all my orders and, whatever I command you, you will carry it out blindly to the letter.

'All your plunder, your loot, I leave to you, and in addition I will furnish you with clothing, with arms, and with ammunition, together with a hundred gold ducats, in exchange for which you will hand over to me all the prisoners you take, to dispose of as I choose . . . Do you find my offer acceptable?'

* *Czegenyi legeniek:* (literally 'poor boys'), a gang of hooligans.

'Of course' said the *betyar* with a laugh. 'And I am quite ready to bind myself to the work.'

'In what way?'

'By my oath and solemn promise'.

Thereupon, the brigand held out to the Princess his strong and weather-beaten hand. She took it amicably, and then the *betyar* placed a finger on the crucifix that stood upon Sarolta's praying-stool and swore fidelity and obedience to her. She followed his example and assured him with a solemn oath that she would keep all the promises she had made to him.

Thus was concluded this terrible pact.

Soon all the regions round about were alarmed by the incursions of a band of brigands who, in respect of numbers, armaments, audacity, and particularly as regards acts of cruelty, surpassed everything that had ever been seen before.

Until then, indeed, the depredations of brigands had been tolerated with patience, even, almost, with serenity, as an unavoidable plague. The relations of the "poor boys" with the population were excellent. They never did any harm to people who paid them a tribute in cash or kind and who did not denounce them to the patrols of *pandours*.*

On the highways they pillaged the rich landowners, the bourgeoisie and the priests, but they did not seriously ill-treat any of them. They shed blood only where they met with armed resistance or when someone would have handed them over to the police.

But the day came when this band gave itself up to an orgy of devastation and murders and spared no one: whoever fell into their hands was subjected to hideous tortures, was mutilated and put to death.

Seigniorial castles, convents, monasteries and presbyteries were sacked by them and burned; they destroyed without pity, without mercy, whatever they could not carry off with them. The judges, the local authorities,

* *Pandours:* Hungarian soldiers employed in police duties.

the *pandours* themselves, were powerless to restrain this bloodthirsty horde. Troops had to be called out, but with no better result.

Soon in all the country there was no one to be found who would furnish to the representatives of law and order any useful indication that might lead to the capture of the bandits, or even cast a single glance likely to betray them.

Those people who did, here and there, take the risk of denouncing the band and then fell into their hands, disappeared in an inexplicable way or were found frightfully mutilated and done to death.

Among the peasantry, the strangest and most exaggerated legends became current concerning this terrifying gang, and these even found their echo in the castles and among the authorities of the district.

Rumour had it that these brigands had at their head a woman as beautiful as she was cruel and bloodthirsty, who, having abandoned herself to lascivious games with her victims, put them to death immediately afterwards by means of the most barbarous torments that a heartless and degenerate woman could devise.

Soon this horrible and mysterious creature became known by no other name than "The Hyena of the Plain". Mothers would threaten their children by mentioning her name, and no one doubted but that she hid her face under a black mask. That, at any rate, is what trembling husbands continually told their wives, lovers their mistresses, brothers their sisters...

Chapter IX

In the Net

The year of mourning had gone by and still the Princess Parkany seemed to be in the grip of the profoundest sadness as a result of the death of her husband, and still affected such mortification that she seemed unable to bring herself to have anything to do with the outside world.

At last, she began to visit her neighbours and receive visits from them, and then she took a further step and issued invitations, first to intimate dinner parties, and then at last to great *soirées* and hunts.

Finally, as winter was covering the earth with a mantle of snow, she organised sleigh parties, and whips cracked, shotgun reports were heard, champagne corks popped joyously once more at Parkany as in the old days when its noble proprietor was still alive.

After her marriage to the Prince, among all the aristocratic families in the country Sarolta had become intimately linked only with a certain Countess Baratony, a rich and intellectual widow of some fifty years, and her two daughters.

One December afternoon, when it was freezing hard outside, Sarolta was sitting by the fireplace in the ancestral long room of the Baratony castle with the three ladies, and all four, as they chatted, were smoking cigarettes which the Princess rolled most adroitly with choice Turkish tobacco.

While this was going on, a parlour-maid handed the mistress of the castle a silver tray bearing a visiting-card, which the lady read without ceremony: 'Baron von Steinfeld.'

Sarolta began to tremble and her lips blanched. Then, pulling herself together: 'Steinfeld?' said she. 'Isn't that the gentleman who some time ago was the victim of an attempt on his life?'

'The same', replied the Countess. 'He was very gravely injured in an absolutely baffling manner at the side of his wife, but, thanks to the skill of a doctor, he managed to recover.'

It was the Baron himself who was to supply further explanations. Since that catastrophe which had all but cost him his life at the Goldrain castle, Steinfeld had singularly aged.

His hair and the whole beard which he now wore had turned completely grey; his wan face was furrowed with deep wrinkles engraved by the fate he had endured; his bearing had changed and had become completly stiff and unbending. Only his eyes still retained the gleam of the old days.

On the other hand, his former mistress still seemed almost as young as ever. It would have been difficult readily to establish any link between Anna Klauer, the daughter of poor working-class people who later became the mistress of the Baron, and the Princess Sarolta Parkany: the golden-blonde hair of the Princess gave her a completely different expression, even more voluptuous, due to the fact that her complexion had become more delicate, more sombre.

Finally, her superb breasts seemed to be even more fully formed and more majestic. For these reasons Baron Steinfeld was unable to recognise her, and the more so since she abstained from saying very much and, in any case, her voice had lost its early immaturity and instead of the charming Viennese dialect she now spoke the beautiful but cold Hanoverian tongue. The conversation rapidly became of the most animated kind. From it Sarolta learned that Steinfeld had bought the property situated near Kurzem, adjoining the estates of the Countess, and there he had set up his home, together with his wife and the two daughters she had borne him; she soon guessed that he was not happy in his domestic life and that their union had been troubled by gloomy regrets which had robbed him of all his illusions.

As soon as the Princess had convinced herself that Steinfeld did not recognise her, did not even suspect that it was she he was looking at, she began with audacious dexterity to let fly at him all the arrows of her flirtatiousness. Steinfeld, who, from the very first moment, had felt dazzled by the devilish beauty of the Princess, allowed himself to be more and more captivated at every glance that those deep and dominating eyes cast in his direction.

After having seen himself more than once deceived in his ideals, or, through his own passions, let himself be led to the very edge of the abyss, the Baron, like all sophisticated men who are fatigued by enjoyments, had reached the stage when a sweet, good and affectionate wife no longer offers any attraction, when jaded nerves desire at any price excitement and fantasy, when nothing can excite or inflame except the torments which a heartless, coquettish and cruel woman inflicts upon a man weak enough to become in reality, as well as figuratively, her stepping-stone, and when life yields enjoyment and pleasure by the very reason of the perfidy of the beloved one.

In contrast to the fidelity and affection of his wife, whose love confined itself to evincing all that which constitutes the practice of domestic virtues, for Baron Steinfeld the hate and scorn of a selfish and haughty woman would have been a real delight and consolation, and he felt his head turned by the bursts of provocative laughter and the flattering words of Sarolta.

He sensed in her one of those imperious, passionate, pitiless natures that conveyed to him all he now longed for, and he conceived the idea that she was clearly exhorting him to make advances to her. That thought made him thrill with joy, like a child being petted.

The Princess, when she took leave of him, did so in the most amiable manner, and invited him to come and visit her; he thanked her delightedly, but with unmistakable awkwardness. However, even before he was able to avail himself of the permission which Sarolta had granted him to pay her a visit, a mounted hussar brought him, for himself and his wife, an invitation from the Princess to take part in a wolf-hunt which she was holding at Parkany.

On the day arranged, all the nobility of the neighbourhood forgathered at the late Prince's castle: ladies and gentlemen dressed in their rich silks in the Hungarian style, arrived from all parts in fantastic sleighs representing swans, lions, griffins or dragons breathing fire.

163

It had been decided that in order to be protected and looked after, each lady would be accompanied by a cavalier drawn by lot; each sleigh would contain two couples. Nevertheless, it was not chance alone that decided that Baron Steinfeld and his wife would be the companions of the Princess.

As the couples got under way in the race to reach the forest where the wolves had been rounded up, following a *battue*, and caught in snares, the Baron was seized by a feeling of shame at having allowed, even reluctantly, the female demon that was Sarolta to take her place in the same sleigh as his own wife.

The discreet little Baroness looked literally frozen, despite her thick fur-lined jacked; her fur bonnet made her look old, and she huddled so timorously where she sat, with a certain nobleman called Ürmeny, that she could inspire no other sentiment than pity.

By contrast, the Princess, wrapped in her rich ermine fur coat lined with black velvet, her *katschma* of the same fur coquettishly poised on her coiffured curls, looked radiant in her superb beauty and as if positively enthroned among the sleek bearskins.

The cold only made the fluorescent freshness of her face more pronounced and she drove the team with her own hands with the elegance and self-confidence of a true Amazon.

The hunt began.

The hunters established themselves along one of the borders of the wood, then the wire meshes were raised on this side and hundreds of beaters, shouting at the tops of their voices, began to drive the panic-stricken animals before them in the direction of the hunters.

'You have no gun, Princess', said the Baron to Sarolta. 'Have you no wish to shoot? Do you feel pity for these wild creatures?'

The beautiful woman chuckled.

'On the contrary, I am only waiting for the moment when the wolves come out of the wood, to leap into the saddle and hurl myself upon them with my dogs, that's where the real pleasure of the hunt comes in: when you give the beast the chance to escape. When they have used up all their strength and all their ruses to try to save themselves, and when, at last, they see they are hemmed in on all sides, they come back to the snares and, quivering and in agony, await the *coup de grâce*.

'And that is how I myself look upon love.'

'You are a strange, extraordinary woman', murmured the Baron. 'You inspire in a man a kind of fearfulness of which he becomes more and more aware, thanks to the magic and diabolical power you exercise over him.'

'And could that be the effect I have produced on *you*?' asked Sarolta, looking at Steinfeld with her great calm eyes and piercing him, so to speak, to the depths of his soul.

He quivered under her stare and could not find a word to say in reply.

'You are silent', said the Princess with a laugh.

That laugh disconcerted the Baron even more than the woman's look.

She added: 'I can now read in your face the answer to my question. Dare I tell you what I think? You are comparing me to your dear dainty little wife, and you are saying to yourself that you would experience infinitely greater delight in being my slave than you find in being her master.'

'Princess! Me?...' stammered Steinfeld.

'You can hide nothing from me', continued Sarolta. 'Not even your most secret thoughts. You are not happy: your wife leads you by the nose and by the ears ...'

'And even if that were true?...' said the Baron uncomfortably.

'Oh, come now, calm yourself', replied the Princess with such complete assurance that she disarmed the Baron. 'You must preserve that pleasure, and share it with all the sufferings that go with it, all the sufferings that such a woman can inflict on a man like you, crazily fond of illusions, unhappy though you are.

'Your wife is unable to gratify your wishful thinking.

Now as for me, I might still be able, Baron, if you loved me, if you adored me, I could still, I say, laugh at you like hell, when the devil triumphs... But it seems to me it is time now to mount our horses. The wolves are coming. Do you see?'

At that, Sarolta leapt down from the sleigh and on to the back of her Arab steed, even before the Baron had had time to offer her his assistance. He found a horse all ready and waiting for him.

Hardly had he mounted when the dogs were released and the chase began.

In vain did the wolf, who was exposed to the bullets of the hunters, try to evade them and regain his liberty, to escape his pursuers. After a frantic chase of almost four hours, he flung himself into the palisades leading to the wolf-pits, but already the Princess was there. The creature tried vainly to elude the pursuit of which he was the object. The dogs seized him inside the enclosure and began to tear him to pieces.

Sarolta leapt briskly down from her horse and, her eyes sparkling with a bloodthirsty delight, plunged her *yatagan** into his throat.

As the wolf fell dead at the Princess's feet, Steinfeld, who had just dismounted, remarked to Sarolta: 'This scene has for me a symbolic significance. Something inside me tells me that it is this same fate that awaits me. Could this be a presage do you think?'

'You're too late', said Sarolta mischievously. 'You are caught already. I have you in my net, and all that remains to do is to give *you* the *coup de grâce*!'

Chapter X
THE BLOOD BATH

Baron Steinfeld was now a regular dinner guest at the Parkany castle.

Sarolta amused herself with him in so improbable and

* *Yatag(h)an:* Mohammedan pointed sword with double-curved blade.

166

refined a manner that in this blasé man, whose whims paralysed his will-power, whose spirits seemed annihilated, the prime ardour of youth revived only under the dominion of the strange passion she inspired, and only that passion could bring to life a heart buried under the lava of years gone by.

He loved the Princess Parkany as he had never loved either his own wife or even Anna Klauer, but the more she gave him to understand that he had no place in her life, not even the smallest, that every hour she granted him he was stealing from her like a common and persistent beggar, the more he pleaded for her love, even though he felt that his presence was a source of irritation to her.

Sarolta gloated over the tortures she inflicted upon him in this way, and nothing could equal the enjoyment that she derived from him when, while she reclined on a velvety couch, he grovelled in the dust and fervently applied his lips to the Princess's feet, entreating, sighing and weeping for a single word of love.

Then, she would laugh and push him away with her foot, or else, seizing the whip that she used for her hounds, she would strike him like a slave—no, like a dog—and he enjoyed this ill-treatment as he had never done when smothered with love and kisses in the arms of his wife.

When Sarolta had driven him to a state bordering on insanity and he had threatened to take his own life if she would not listen to his entreaties, she pointed out to him with haughty frigidity that she was not the woman to share a man's heart with others, and imposed, as a condition for her favours, the only one that she could decently accept, that is to say to take the place of his wife and his children. She wanted by this insistence not to precipitate her act of vengeance, but on the contrary to savour it slowly, step by step.

Steinfeld was ready to make any sacrifice; his only thought was to possess the beautiful and demoniacal woman: he wanted nothing else.

He left for Pest; at home he lacked the courage to convey personally to his wife the crushing declaration that he did not love her, that he never had loved her, and that he felt incapable of living with her any longer.

He did so by letter, the terms of which had been dictated by Sarolta herself. At the same time, he assigned to his wife and children as a residence the castle of Goldrain in Bohemia.

The poor little woman fainted when she read the letter, and spent three days and three nights in a crisis of weeping, during which time she did not even undress. Then, she made her preparations to depart.

As she was getting into her carriage with her children, Sarolta suddenly appeared before her and shouted: 'Bon voyage, Baroness! Before you leave these parts, you should know who is driving you away. It is I who have stolen your husband's heart. This is poetic justice. You deprived the poor working-class girl, Anna Klauer, of her happiness and drove her into the path of vice and crime, and now Princess Parkany has paid you back. Bon voyage!'

The day following the departure of his wife and children, Baron Steinfeld returned to his residence and wrote Sarolta a letter full of feverish desires, in which he reminded her of her promise and called upon her to carry it out.

'Whatever promise I have made I will keep', was the Princess's reply. 'I am yours. Come tonight about 10 o'clock. My confidential maid will be expecting you at the small back door and will conduct you to my bedchamber.'

Steinfeld kissed the letter more than a hundred times: he could not stop covering it with kisses, and was in a state of utter jubilation the like of which he had never known in all his life.

In his reveries he already saw himself as the conqueror of the most desirable woman in the world and his imagination depicted the conquest of the haughty Sarolta in the most romantic colours.

He had never before given so much care to his toilet as he did today. His old valet had rarely seen him so impatient; nothing went right: five times he pulled off his cravat and put on another. At last he was ready. He still had an hour before him in which to get to Parkany. That hour seemed to him like a century.

He picked up the first book that came to hand. It was a book about the mysteries of Paris, and Steinfeld read a scene in it in which, through her cruel artifices, a pretty Creole girl made of her admirer the implacable partisan of a sensuality bordering on madness.

The Baron was intoxicated by this picture and it seemed to him that it must be a sort of enjoyment to fall into the hands of so pitiless a woman. He did not suspect that he himself was about to experience a similar fate.

After a while he threw the novel on one side and made his way to the stables where he saddled his horse himself. This done, he went to the servants' quarters and chatted with them while smoking a cigar.

At last, the castle clock struck nine.

The Baron leapt into his saddle and spurred his horse in both flanks. The sweetest images came into his mind and as he rode along: in his imagination he saw Sarolta awaiting him, dressed in a wedding-gown. His heart pounded, the throbbing of his pulse increased tenfold.

He had eyes for nothing to right or left; all his attention was concentrated upon himself. When he was half-way there, he came to a chapel that had been erected on the very spot where a rich burgess had been assassinated by brigands.

At that very moment, two shots rang out; Steinfeld's horse fell dead and the Baron himself was trapped underneath the animal and lay completely at the mercy of men with blackened faces who had sprung out upon him from a nearby thicket and had no trouble in overpowering him and binding him. He was left in no doubt but that he had fallen into the hands of bandits and he took his fate philosophically.

'I say, you poor fellows', he exclaimed, 'let me go free and you shall gain a large sum of money. I am awaited by a beautiful woman and you will readily understand that for me it is a most disagreeable mischance to have fallen into your hands!'

The brigands began to laugh and one of them, who seemed to be their leader, said to him:

'We can't let you go, Baron, but we are going to take you right away to a pretty woman all the same.'

'How so?'

'You know her very well, at least by reputation', said the bandit in a jocular tone. 'The people hereabouts call her the Hyena of the Plain.'

'For the love of God', pleaded the Baron, 'have pity on me!'

But the brigands would no more let themselves be softened by his supplications than tempted by the sums of money he offered to lavish upon them; they gagged him, threw a cloth over his head, mounted him upon a horse, and rode off with him at a mad pace . . .

When his bonds had been removed and the cloth and the gag taken away, Baron Steinfeld found himself in a vaulted room, without windows, the architecture of which resembled that of medieval citadels, but the luxurious furnishings of which suggested the boudoir of a great lady.

The person who had brought Steinfeld here left him in this room and slammed the heavy iron door behind him. However, the Baron did not remain long alone. Soon he heard in the next room the rustle of a woman's dress, then the heavy curtain concealing the door parted.

A tall and majestic woman, all dressed in black velvet, covered with a veil, her face concealed by a black velvet mask, entered, and surveyed the Baron with a look that froze the blood in his veins.

'Do you recognise me?' said a well-known voice.

'Princess!' exclaimed Steinfeld, suddenly relieved of all anxiety. 'It's you! So all this is just a joke?'

'There's no joke about it, Baron, but a terrifying reality', replied the masked lady. 'Do you *really* know who I am?'

'No!'

'Very well, then I am going to come to your miserable

aid!' exclaimed she, tearing off her mask and throwing aside her veil.

It was indeed the Princess, but she had dyed her hair black, and Steinfeld recognised her at once.

'Anna Klauer!' he faltered, terror-stricken.

'Yes, Anna Klauer', she said, her arms folded on her breast; 'the poor working girl whom you seduced, whom you well and truly ravished, corrupted by your luxury, only to abandon her afterwards and consign her to a life of vice.

'That Anna Klauer who drowned her child and yours, who almost at Goldrain took away your life with a pistol!

'Now the redoubtable Sarolta Parkany, who poisoned her husband and has allied herself with brigands for the sweet pleasure of taking revenge on men, and above all on you!

'Look at me closely! I am the woman who makes thousands of people tremble, whom everyone thinks capable of the most bloodthirsty acts, all forms of cruelty,—the Hyena of the Plain.'

'Mercy! Mercy!...' implored the Baron, falling upon his knees.

Her only reply was a burst of hateful and pitiless laughter, and as she laughed she clapped her hands. At once her two servants Ersabeth and Iela, both dressed in blood-red velvet, rushed from the next room, seized Steinfeld, bound his hands behind his back, and then put irons on his feet.

'What are you going to do to me?' asked the poor wretch, trembling in all his limbs.

'Judge you!' she replied with demoniacal majesty.

'You are going to kill me!' he exclaimed.

'Surely, but I intend that you shall die gradually', she said balefully. 'A dagger thrust or a draught of poison would be too quick a relief for you: that could not satisfy me.'

'Have pity on me, Anna; I will put everything right', groaned Steinfeld.

She would not listen to him. At a glance from her, the wenches dragged him into the next room, which was in all respects like a torture-chamber and in one corner of which stood a marble bath or font that four steps led up to.

Sarolta reclined carelessly on a couch that stood nearby, then she said to the girls:

'Do what I have commanded you and don't ask me anything more, so that I may feast my eyes in tranquillity on the sufferings of this wretch!'

The two wenches lifted Steinfeld up and suspended him from a hook, after having brought his arms from behind his back, in such a way that, his feet off the ground, he hung stretched like a prisoner on the rack; then they placed under him a great stove in which they lit a big fire.

Until now, the Hyena's victim had not uttered any sound of complaint; but as the flames began to lick the soles of his feet, he emitted first a slight sigh and wept with pain, then began to howl and rave like a madman.

His distended nerves could not endure this torment. Nevertheless he had to, and all the while, the more he roared in the delirium of suffering, the more the cruel woman laughed, lying on the couch, and the more the two hideous vixens stoked the fire.

When at last they released him, he fell to the ground like a lump of wood.

'I can stand no more. Let me die!'

'Not yet', cried the girls.

They seemed to experience savage delight in martyrising the poor defenceless victim. They laid Steinfeld on his back and chained him solidly to the floor. Then they applied to each foot the Iron Boot, the most hideous instrument of torture that the imagination of the Spanish Inquisitors ever invented.

They untied his hands, and then placed his fingers in thumb-screws, till blood spurted from under his nails. Fortunately for him, he lost consciousness.

The old hag was called. She tended him a little, then said:

'Finish him off, Sarolta, my sweet little dove. He is very low. He can't last much longer!'

'But I don't want to!' exclaimed the beautiful Hyena, stamping her foot with rage.

'Then he will be dead too soon', replied the witch.

'Oh, all right then, stop!' Sarolta ordered her two female executioners, who removed one by one the instruments of torture and released Steinfeld.

'Use all the resources of your art, old woman, to revive him. He must recover consciousness and remain conscious until the end.'

The sorceress came back with all kinds of phials and flasks and soon set to work at the task. After a number of attentions, Steinfeld's eyelids fluttered and he looked at her.

'That didn't cost you your life, did it?' exclaimed Sarolta. 'But you have atoned enough and now the most beautiful reward awaits you. Come to me, I want to be merciful and give you your life and give myself to you. Come, we shall celebrate our wedding.'

'Can this be true, Anna? No more cruelties?' asked Steinfeld, as if recovering from a bad dream.

'Don't ask me anything more. I am yours', exclaimed the beautiful woman, holding out her arms to him.

He tried to approach, but fell down before he could reach her. The girls picked him up and placed him at Sarolta's feet.

'So you are mine?' stammered the Baron, as she put her superb arms around him and kissed him.

With a glance she dismissed the two servants. The old hag laid a costly sable fur coat by the Princess's head on the cushion of the couch and retired also.

'I want to make myself more beautiful', said Sarolta with a gay laugh, 'as beautiful as Venus Anadyomene.'

Steinfeld helped her to undress and then handed her the sable fur in which she wrapped herself with inimitable grace and which reached to the soles of her feet; then she pressed her diabolical lips against his until, crazy with joy, he fell at her feet.

'Finish me off', he implored her in sudden ecstasy.

'Indeed I will', said Sarolta with a sinister look.

She made a slight sound and, in the twinkling of an eye, Steinfeld was once again seized by the servants, who then chained him to an iron ring fixed in the wall above the marble font.

'What does this mean?' he shouted. 'What has come over you?'

'You will soon find out', said Sarolta, rising.

Then the servants tore off all his clothes.

'You robbed me of my youth, you swine', continued Sarolta, 'and now you shall pay it back with your own blood!'

'What? Am I mad?'

'Have you never heard of that Hungarian Countess who took baths in human blood and so remained eternally young? Today I want to experiment with that strange beauty secret.'

'My God! Can this be possible?' groaned Steinfeld. 'Surely I must be dreaming!'

'Then wake up!' exclaimed the beautiful Hyena.

She threw off her fur coat and climbed into the marble font.

The two servants advanced upon the poor wretch, each of them armed with a whip, with sharp steel-pointed thongs similar to those used by the Inquisition, and began their cruel task.

After a few lashes, their victim was completely lacerated, his blood flowing in streams into the font below, inundating the beautiful woman who voluptuously plunged her superb limbs in the warm life-blood and chuckled each time that Steinfeld howled like one possessed.

Soon he could utter only faint sighs, and at last there hung from the ring an inert mass, bleeding and lifeless.

Anna Klauer was revenged ...

"...their victim was completely lacerated, his blood...
innudating the beautiful woman..."

Chapter XI

A Delilah of the People

Once again there was a bloody night at Parkany. The brigands had brought in Father Pistian, whom they dragged into the Hyena's den, where first he enjoyed Sarolta's favours, and then had to pay for them with the most frightful torments and at last with his own blood.

After this horrible bath, the Princess, draped in dark furs, lay on the sofa and was massaged by old Halka with mysterious essences.

'Now, my dove', mumbled the sorceress, 'do you find the use of my methods satisfactory? Do you feel the vivifying and rejuvenating effects?'

'I certainly do, and I am grateful to you. I have the greatest confidence in the world in you', replied Sarolta, staring at her with a sombre expression.

'But what does this mean?' said the old woman. 'More than ever your body is blooming with new youth and yet more than ever your soul is invaded by the deepest shadows. Are you not content?'

'No, Halka, you are right', replied the Hyena with a sigh. 'Love claims its dues, and I love till I hate, but I love in vain.'

'Can this be?'

'It's the honest truth', mumured Sarolta. 'I have loved Emerich Bethlemy ever since I first saw him, and he . . . he scorns me.'

'Who told you that?'

'I have offered him my hand . . . '

'And he has refused you', said the old woman with a sly cackle. 'Believe me, for you must know men,—give him a taste of the whip and he will kiss your feet.'

'It is too late to put that to the test.'

'Have them seize him, my little one!' exclaimed the witch, 'and we shall see whether we cannot tame that heedless young fellow.'

'You are right, Halka. Yes, we will do that', replied the Princess. 'Is Eyula still in the castle?'

'Certainly. You have not given him your orders for tomorrow.'

'Call him then.'

The witch went out and came back soon with the *betyar*.

'Listen, Eyula', began the Princess. 'You must bring me young Emerich Bethlemy tomorrow without fail.'

'Nothing could be more simple', replied the brigand. 'It's a job that I'll find pleasing, the more so because no one has done more than he has to hinder our work. He is always dashing off to Pest and going to complain to the Commissariat who, he says, are too lukewarm and do not bring enough severity or vigour to bear in trying to suppress us. As far as I am concerned, he must be punished in an exemplary fashion.'

'But how will you seize him? How will you capture him?' enquired Sarolta. 'He is sure to be on his guard.'

'I know a servant-girl named Ursa', replied the brigand, 'who has often done us little services already. She is a naughty and a wanton little devil, to tell the truth, but as beautiful and tricky as a grass-snake; she'll hand him over to us for a few jingling crowns, that goes without saying.'

'How so?'

'She's his mistress.'

'A creature like that!' murmured Sarolta. 'And yet he scorns me! I want to talk to his girl myself, Eyula. Take me to her now, at once.'

The girl lived with her aged mother in the middle of the plain, in a tavern that was almost in ruins, where she sold *eau-de-vie* and wine and where she cooked a meal for anyone who asked for it.

All sorts of people came there: hawkers, Jews on their

way to some market, *pandours*, wandering gypsies, harlots, and thieves.

She was accustomed to getting up at any hour of the night and it did not surprise her in the least when there was a knock at the door after midnight and when three masked men, armed from head to foot, pushed their way in and demanded to be served with something good to drink.

When they had sat down and she had been to fetch a bottle of old wine which she placed before them, one of the thieves who, to judge from his appearance and his clothing, seemed to be the youngest and the most distinguished of the band, put his arms around her waist and said:

'Well my pretty one, would you like to please me?'

'Why not?' replied the girl, a passionate and really beautiful Hungarian lass, but on whose features there was set the seal of the most depraved forms of debauchery.

Thereupon, she summed up her questioner, while her strong hand stroked the broad fur with which his *attila*** was richly bordered, and it struck her that the person who was sitting before her could not be a thief, but must be some wealthy and handsome young man.

'One who pays you well and also makes you a little present on the side ought to be very kindly received, Ursa', exclaimed one of the handsome young man's companions.

'All right! What do you want of me?' laughed the beautiful and mischievous creature, at the same time sitting on the lap of the man with the fur-trimmed jacket. 'Do you want to go to bed with me?'

'You are a very pretty girl, Ursa', replied the other, 'but that's not quite what I want. I want something better than that: you must arrange to see your lover tomorrow night—young Bethlemy—and give up your place to me.'

'And that's what you call better?' said the girl roguishly.

'Of course, Ursa, because you see I too am a woman.'

'You must be joking.'

---

* *Attila:* Hungarian jacket.

'No, I am not joking. Have you never heard of the Hyena of the Plain?'

Ursa bounded up and dashed into a corner with a startled cry.

'Come now, don't be afraid', said Sarolta, getting up and following Ursa. 'Yes, I am that dreadful woman of whom all Hungary talks in fear and trembling, but, in spite of that, we shall be the best friends in the world if you consent to deliver Bethlemy to me.'

'What do you want to do with him?' asked Ursa.

'Amuse myself a little with him and then . . . '

'Kill him?'

'*You* said it.'

The girl thought for a moment, and then asked:

'What will you give me?'

'Twenty ducats here and now', replied Sarolta, 'and this bracelet too.'

She pulled back the sleeve of her fur jacket and took from her arm a gold band in the centre of which sparkled a ruby, and she placed it on the arm of the girl. Then she said:

'There will be another 20 ducats for you when it is all over.'

'All right', sighed the girl as she stared at the sparkling bracelet. 'I'll do what you ask.'

The next night Bethlemy did indeed make his way on horseback to the tavern and there he found sitting in the tavern lounge Ursa's old mother, together with two strangers.

As he entered, the old woman got up and whispered in his ear that Ursa was waiting for him in her bedroom, that all he had to do was join her there, but, although she said this in a hushed polite tone, she made it obvious that every word could be heard. Now, as Bethlemy knew that Ursa never willingly permitted any facetiousness or flippancy concerning her love-making, he left the inn at once, mounted his horse and made as if to return the way he had come.

A few hundred paces from the tavern, he returned to it, tied his horse to a willow-tree and, going round the back, climbed the narrow, steep staircase.

Hardly had his foot touched the threshold of the dark room when he felt himself seized by two strong arms with a vigour such as he had never yet known with Ursa, and before he could recover his breath he was drawn into a passionate embrace and hugged against superbly formed breasts while two lips burning with desire fastened on his mouth . . .

As the stars were beginning to fade in the firmament and the first warm rays of the rising light of day began to throw their pale glow into the room, Bethlemy, voluptuously kissing the woman at his side, told her:

'And now I am afraid we must part!'

'Never, Bethlemy!' replied a voice that seemed strange to him and yet that he seemed at once to recognise, although not as the voice of Ursa. 'Never!' the voice repeated. 'You are mine, mine for all time, or till death—if you prefer!'

'Who are you?' murmured the young nobleman. 'Who talks to me like this? Ursa, where are you?'

'I am not Ursa, but the one you have just been kissing and making love to!' said the woman at his side, and then she burst into a playful laugh.

'You, my God!' stammered Bethlemy. 'That voice! . . . Can it be possible! . . .'

'I am she whom you have scorned, and who still loves you', she said with majestic calm,—'Sarolta, Princess Parkany!'

Bethlemy was dismayed, and recoiled.

'I am going to be frank with you', continued the Princess.

Thereupon she got up slowly, put on her feet a pair of slippers trimmed with fur and wrapped herself in a sable pelisse. Then she went on:

'I love you and I want to possess you—at any price— and for that I am determined to kill you rather than let any other woman have you. Do you understand me, my friend?'

'I understand that I have been deceived and betrayed in an odious fashion.'

' "Sold" would be the most appropriate expression', said Sarolta mockingly. 'Until now you were the lover of a common prostitute with whom you had relations in this room; she sold you to me, so that now you belong to me like a slave I might have bought in the market.'

'Appalling!' exclaimed the young gentleman.

'Stay with me', went on the Princess. 'I love you; resign yourself to your fate. Surely, after all, it's not so terrible as you seem to think. Am I not rich and distinguished? Am I not beautiful?'

'You are the most beautiful woman I have ever seen', exclaimed Bethlemy, 'and yet I cannot love you. There's something in your face that puts me off you; the mark of Cain seems to be imprinted on your forehead, your hands seem stained with blood. I cannot love you.'

'Try', replied the beautiful woman, 'I beg you. I love you so much; I have never loved anyone as I love you.'

She got up, put her arms around his neck and kissed him.

He did not move away from her, but remained still.

'Come with me to Parkany', she continued. 'Forget the wretch that has betrayed you. Be mine. Try, if only for a short time—a week, a day even . . . '

'No, no!' replied Bethlemy. 'Not even for an hour. Your beauty might intoxicate my senses, but my heart would abhor you. I cannot love you.'

At that very moment, Eyula appeared in the doorway.

'Day is beginning to break', he cried. 'Make haste, Princess, otherwise we shall fall into the hands of the *pandours.*'

'My God!' exclaimed Bethlemy. 'My presentiment was well-founded: I knew you were a villain. You are the chief of this bloodthirsty band. You are the Hyena of the Plain.'

'And if I am', replied Sarolta, 'it is you who have made me so. I ask you for the last time: will you be mine?—

not my husband, nor my lover, but my slave whom I shall trample underfoot,—or will you die?'

'I prefer to die', exclaimed Bethlemy.

'Leave him to me, the arrogant young rascal!' said Eyula. 'I will make death very hard for him.'

'Take him away', replied Sarolta with an air of indifference that made Bethlemy shudder, 'and do what you like with him.'

She turned her back on him, while Eyula and his companions threw Bethlemy to the floor, bound him, and hurried him outside, taunting him with all kinds of vulgar jests.

Chapter XII

THE ANTS' NEST

Outside the tavern, the brigands hauled their prisoner on to a horse, tied him securely to it, and made off with him across the plain. When they reached a forest of oak trees, they halted there for a couple of hours, lit a fire and set up a camp around it. They seemed to be waiting for someone. They prolonged their stop for a further hour.

All at once, the sound of a galloping horse could be heard in the distance and soon Sarolta herself dismounted. She had again dressed in masculine clothes: high boots, clinging black breeches, and a sort of small *attila* trimmed with sable and ornamented with frogs and loops of gold.

Her beautiful head and her matt complexion were set off by a *kutschma** of sable surmounted by a tuft of heron feathers. One of the brigands hastened to hold her horse while she lightly sprang to the ground and then approached the fire.

'Now come along, hurry yourselves!' she exclaimed. 'It

* *Kutschma:* a Russian type of fur hat.

is broad daylight and *pandours* are about on the plain.'

At that injunction, two brigands pulled their captive off the horse, threw him to the ground like a beast, tied his hands together by means of a long rope, and then dragged him like a package through the forest.

In the course of this short but painful martyrdom, the poor fellow's head banged at every moment against the knotty roots the great oaks had thrown up all around them, or on some of the large sharp stones that were strewn about the forest paths.

He was frightfully disfigured and the blood streamed down his poor face by the time his torturers had halted near a fallen tree trunk, in which a colony of industrious and laborious ants had set up their headquarters. The small black insects were swarming all round, seeking the heat of the sun, and perhaps also to steal a scrap of booty from a neighbouring tribe of their fellow creatures.

The bandits placed Bethlemy head first in the middle of the ants' nest, and rested his body against the thick branch of a young oak that had grown right beside the rotting trunk, and there they tied him securely.

The beautiful Hyena assisted them in the work and gave the keenest approbation to this atrocious and infernal ingenuity.

When the cruel task was finished, the inhuman woman strode up to him and mocked her helpless victim in the most horrible terms. At that moment, Ursa, who had slipped away in haste from the tavern, arrived on the spot.

As for her, she had quickly decided to bestride Bethlemy's horse and had hastened to warn them they were being pursued, more in order to prevent their suspecting that she had betrayed them than because it mattered to her to save these ferocious companions.

'What is this you are doing?' she said in astonishment, as soon as she perceived Bethlemy in his strange position.

'We are assisting the noble lord to get to heaven', replied Eyula.

'How so?'

'Is this method so new to you, Ursa?' asked another brigand. 'I understand that this sort of thing must have happened a good many times before here on the plain.'

'This is the first time I have seen it', said the girl, looking down at her betrayed lover with the most cold and heartless curiosity.

'Come then, I am going to show you something you don't know', replied Eyula. 'See here, my girl, this is an ants' nest which we have shoved the cavalier in.

'Not long after we have left this place, the dear little creatures will be sure to see him for the first time and will proceed to treat him exactly as they have treated this block of oak that they have completely gnawed away. Instead of inhabiting a commonplace lump of wood, they will establish their residence in a fine noble skull.'

'But that's frightful!' murmured Ursa in a tone of frigid indifference.

'For him, perhaps!' said the *betyar* in a mocking tone. 'He probably even has a slight headache already. I once heard a monk whom we had treated in this way yell like a real raving lunatic. It was very funny! It's a great pity that we cannot hear this one!'

'How long does it take for death to come?' the girl asked.

'Oh, quite a long time', replied the brigand; 'two or three days.'

'You're a masterly fellow!' exclaimed Sarolta. 'Here's something for your delightful and brilliant inventiveness.'

She took a great fistful of ducats and slipped them into the bandit's hand, and then added: 'But now to horse, otherwise we shall all be in danger ourselves.'

In the twinkling of an eye they were all in the saddle and rode away one after the other.

Bethlemy found himself alone, delivered without hope to the worst of tortures, to the most frightful of deaths; he could feel the ants, first one by one, then in really large numbers, going up and down over his face, as if led by a guide, and then they began to penetrate his ears.

In his unspeakable despair, he began to do what he had not done for many long, long years: he began to pray. He shed tears before God, not for deliverance, but for salvation and a quick death.

Suddenly, he heard footsteps approaching closer and closer, and at last Ursa appeared before the unfortunate fellow. She tapped his face lightly with her open hand and said with a laugh: 'Now, how do you feel, Emerich?'

Bethlemy said nothing.

'Could you still be foolish enough to love me? Tell me.'

'You've sold me and betrayed me, Ursa, and repaid my love with infinite ingratitude', he replied in a tone full of gentleness, 'but I forgive you.'

'Do you really?' she said, laughing gaily.

'I forgive you!'

'Because you think I am going to spare your life.'

'I don't wish to live any more', Bethlemy continued. 'Now that you, whom I love so much, have delivered me to my enemies, death seems to me like a friend; but I beg you, if your heart retains some compassion, some humanity still, kill me now!'

The girl began to giggle again, and, still laughing, drew a long knife from her belt, and then . . . slashed the ties that bound her lover. He was free.

At once Ursa helped him to extricate himself and to get rid of the ants that teemed all over his head.

'I thank you, Ursa,' said Bethlemy, surprised and touched at the same time by the generosity of his treacherous mistress.

'You have nothing to thank me for', she said, still apparently enjoying the situation. 'I have what's left of my money in my pocket and I have brought it to you. But now we must make a quick decision and lose no time in carrying it out, otherwise, before sunset, it will be me who will be the brigands' victim.'

Then she archly kissed her old admirer, set off in haste and disappeared at once into the brushwood.

Chapter XIII

Unmasked

Towards evening the girl returned to the tavern. As she entered the public bar, in which her mother was pouring a drink for a man dressed in a shaggy *bunda** she moved about fearlessly, her head held high, a playful smile at her lips.

She knew that the man who seemed to be trying to size her up belonged to the Hyena's gang and that he was spying on her, but this did not worry her in the least; she sat herself down beside him and began to hum a cheerful song.

'Have you heard, Ursa', said the bandit, 'that Bethlemy, whom we shoved into an anthill this morning, escaped in some extraordinary, miraculous way?'

'I knows he's escaped', replied Ursa with the greatest indifference in the world, 'but I don't see anything very extraordinary in that, considering it was me who let him go.'

'You? But do you realise what you have done?' said the brigand, whose astonishment was far from being entirely feigned.

Over the man's shoulder the old woman cast a meaningful glance at her daughter as if to say: Be careful! But the girl paid no heed to it.

'Aren't you afraid of the Hyena's revenge?' urged the bandit.

'Huh! I don't care a damn about her,' said Ursa. 'Tonight is the last I shall spend under this roof; tomorrow, first thing in the morning, my mother and I will be leaving not only this district, but our country and we shall

* *Bunda:* a kind of Hungarian mantle or cloak.

go, with Bethlemy who owes his life to me and loves me more than ever, to America.'

'That's very wise of you!' replied the brigand, smiling in a strange and sinister way. Thereupon, he got up, paid for his drink and stalked out rapidly.

'What have you done?' said her mother. 'Now we are lost!'

'On the contrary, I know very well what I have done', the girl replied calmly.

Night had just fallen. The old woman had gone up to the room above and was saying her prayers, while Ursa was humming and singing at the top of her voice. Suddenly, there was a knock at the door.

'Who is that?' asked the girl.

'One who will pay his way', was the reply.

'I know who you are, you're Eyula', replied Ursa. 'I have been expecting you, you and your men, because really and truly it's my turn today to treat you...'

'Open up!' yelled twenty voices at once.

'Oh, willingly!' replied Ursa slyly. 'Are you in such a hurry then?'

At the same moment that the door opened and that Eyula, with his face blackened, appeared on the threshold, a shot come from the room and laid him stone dead on the floor; this rifle shot was a signal for the *gendarmes* concealed in the inn to open fire all together on the bandits, through all the windows and the skylights and garret-windows in the roof.

The robbers, dismayed by such a sudden attack, recoiled and broke up, leaving the majority of them killed or wounded, but they quickly came back, and laid siege to the humble shack from all sides.

Some of them even managed to get inside the inn where they waged a bloody hand-to-hand battle with the *pandours;* but very soon there could be heard the galloping of hussars, requisitioned from the neighbouring town by the supreme magistrate of the Commissariat, and who had been hiding in the nearby woods.

The brigands now found themselves caught in a cross-fire. They took to flight, pursued by the hussars, who cut down most of them with their sabres, and took five prisoners. Only two of the brigands succeeded in getting away.

One of these was the chief of this redoubtable band: the vicious Hyena of the Plain herself.

The brigands who had been taken prisoner, in conformity with the cruel but simple and practical method applied by Commissioner Stefan Mad, were forthwith put to the torture until they admitted that the leader of their band was none other than a woman, and that woman was the Princess Sarolta Parkany, which information had previously been supplied already by Ursa.

Thereupon, the Commissioner set off in haste for the Princess's castle, which had, as the tavern had previously, been prudently surrounded. There he enquired the reasons for the Princess's absence.

As he intended to interrogate the three women confidantes, Halka, Iela and Ersabeth, he made an exploration of the castle, and, in the little room in the tower, the door of which he was obliged to force open, he discovered only their corpses.

They had put an end to their criminal existence by taking poison.

Immediately, express messengers, hussars and *pandours* were despatched in all directions to capture the blood-thirsty woman who had ordered and organised all these atrocities. From North to South, from East to West, the telegraph was kept busy. The tocsin sounded in every village.

The common people, incensed against the brigands and their chief, armed themselves with scythes, flails and pitchforks; men, women and children began to scour the forests of the plain, fields and gardens; at morning light the Commissariat's main forces made their appearance.

Towards midday, a group of peasants discovered blood stains beside a marsh, which they immediately surrounded and searched. Suddenly, a shot rang out, followed by a loud shout: everyone ran at once in the direction from which the flash and smoke had been seen; there they found a young man hiding among the reeds, still threatening with his revolver a peasant lying beside him whom he had just felled with a pistol shot.

'Stand back, or I fire!' shouted the young man in a voice which, one felt, was accustomed to command.

But the next moment he was struck across the shoulders a blow with a flail that laid him out on the ground.

The crowd hurled themselves upon him at once, tore away his weapons and tied his hands behind his back.

'Ha, what a fine capture this is!' said an old peasant: 'This is the Princess Parkany herself.'

'The Hyena?' asked twenty voices at once.

'The very same!' the old man affirmed.

'Let's take her to the Commissariat quickly', shouted several people.

'What are you thinking of!' exclaimed the old peasant. 'A brute like this, once taken, must never leave our hands alive. She is tricky enough to send us all to the gallows. She must be killed here and now like a wild beast or a bird of prey...'

'The old man is right. Let's thrash her till she can't move!' shouted the crowd in chorus.

They pulled Sarolta out of the marsh, stripped her of her clothes, and from all sides began to beat her pitilessly with sticks and cudgels.

'Spare my life!' she exclaimed in mortal agony. 'I am rich, very rich, and I will give you everything I possess.'

The blows rained upon her more fiercely than ever. No one seemed to hear her.

'Pity! Have pity!...' she begged.

'Did you have pity on your victims, you wretch?' replied the old peasant. 'Kill her, all of you, without the slightest mercy!'

The peasants went on with their frightful execution. Sarolta had received more than a hundred blows and was bleeding from an almost equal number of wounds; at last she fell unconscious.

'That's enough!' ordered the old man.

'But she's still alive', pleaded a peasant woman.

'That's the point', exclaimed the old man. 'She can't stand any more blows, but we are going to hang her while she's still living.'

'That's it, hang her!' shouted all the crowd...

In vain did Sarolta give vent to the most hideous curses, in vain did she implore mercy, in vain did her mortal anguish and suffering draw tears from her eyes.

A peasant girl struck her a blow on the back of the neck, two other blows fell at once, and after a while her body was swinging from the branch of an alder-tree.

Her death throes lasted only a few minutes, and then this vile female monster gave up the ghost.

The peasants cut down her corpse, threw it on to a dung-cart, and thus she was taken to the Commissariat.